THE GOLDEN THREAD

Der Goldfaden (1557)

THE GOLDEN THREAD

An Agreeable & Entertaining Tale of Lionel, son of a Poor Shepherd, who, by Diligence, Kindness, and Knightly Valor, won the hand of a Nobleman's Daughter: a most useful Narrative for all who love Virtue; written down for Publication by Jörg Wickram, of Colmar.

The First English Translation
by Pierre Kaufke
With an Introduction by Ronald Salter
University of West Florida Press/Pensacola

Copyright 1991 by the Board of Regents of the State of Florida

⊚ Printed in the U.S.A. on acid-free paper.

Wickram, Jörg, ca. 1505-ca. 1560.
 [Goldfaden. English]
 The golden thread : an agreeable & entertaining tale of Lionel, son of a poor shepherd, who, by diligence, kindness, and knightly valor, won the hand of a nobleman's daughter : a most useful narrative for all who love virtue / written down for publication by Jörg Wickram, of Colmar.
   p. cm.
 "Der Goldfaden (1557)."
 Translation of: Der Goldfaden.
 Includes bibliographical references.
 ISBN 0-8130-1045-4
 I. Title.
PT1795.W7G613   1991
833'.4—dc20   90-44258
                                                                  CIP

The University of West Florida Press is a member of University Presses of Florida, the scholarly publishing agency of the State University System of Florida. Books are selected for publication by faculty editorial committees at each of Florida's nine public universities: Florida A & M University (Tallahassee), Florida Atlantic University (Boca Raton), Florida International University (Miami), Florida State University (Tallahassee), University of Central Florida (Orlando), University of Florida (Gainesville), University of North Florida (Jacksonville), University of South Florida (Tampa), and University of West Florida (Pensacola).

Orders for books published by all member presses should be addressed to University Presses of Florida, 15 Northwest 15th Street, Gainesville, Florida 32611.

CONTENTS

Introduction
vii

Translator's Note
xiii

The Golden Thread
1

Select Bibliography
161

Jörg Wickram's Collected Works
165

Editions of *Der Goldfaden*
167

INTRODUCTION

Jörg Wickram, hardly a household name to current American audiences, was one of the most popular writers of his time. And his time was the sixteenth century—a turbulent era of religious strife and social upheaval, of reformatory zeal and political conflict. It was the time when Luther and the peasant wars challenged the seemingly immutable authority of church and state. It was a time of transition and change which witnessed the crumbling of the feudal order under the impact of a new mercantilism and an evolving middle-class culture. All of these circumstances conditioned Wickram's writing.

Little is known about Jörg Wickram's life. Presumed to be an illegitimate child of a local town official, he was born in Colmar (Alsace) shortly after 1500 and was listed as deceased in 1562. By all indications Wickram was a self-educated man of considerable curiosity and energy, a man of many interests and talents in the proverbial Renaissance mode. As a cultural and intellectual leader of his community, he wrote and directed plays for public entertainment; he collected, adapted, and published folktales, poetry, and other kinds of literature; he was active in civil government and in the book trade; he even tried his hand at the visual arts; and he founded a school for the "Meistersang"—an art form of poetry set to music which was developed by the late medieval German guilds in emulation of the courtly love song. His literary productions included "Meisterlieder," Shrovetide farces and religious plays, devotional tracts and didactic pamphlets, short fiction in various forms, and five longer prose works—ranging from derivative adventures in the tradition of knightly romance (*Galmy*, 1539) and the Renaissance novella (*Gabriotto und Reinhart*, 1551) to more realistic depictions of peasant and bourgeois life laced with behavioral models of virtuous conduct (*Der Knabenspiegel*, 1554; *Von guten und bösen Nachbarn*, 1556; *Der Goldfaden*, 1557).

For the German reader, Wickram's literary fame rests largely on his popular *Rollwagenbüchlein* (which had had at least sixteen editions just between 1555 and the outbreak of the Thirty Years' War). Translated roughly as "Stage-Coach Companion" and designed to entertain the traveling reader, it is a collection of short, amusing tales of universal experience with a moral or humorous twist. Duped cuckolds and lascivious priests, clever peasants and dull-witted gentry, pretentious masters and endearing rogues, human foibles and frailties—these are the stock characters and themes of the late-medieval genre known in German as the "Schwank." Related to Boccaccio's and Chaucer's tales, and directed more to the average burgher than to aristocrats and scholars, the Schwank often combined earthy human interest with implicit moral and social instruction.

To entertain and educate the rising middle class was also the purpose of *Der Goldfaden* [*The Golden Thread*], next to the *Rollwagenbüchlein* perhaps Wickram's proudest achievement. The German Romantic poet Brentano admired the novel so much that he translated it in 1809, and Jakob Grimm of fairy-tale fame praised its author as one of the finest writers of the sixteenth century.

The plot of the novel is quickly told. The expected child of a poor but upright Portuguese shepherd is promised to a wealthy merchant whose wife cannot have more than their one child. The newborn Lionel (Lewfried), named for a birthmark of a lion's paw on his chest which is mysteriously connected to the appearance of a peaceful lion among his father's herd, is reared with affection by his foster parents and later sent to school, where he quickly excels through diligence and superior abilities. Unjustly forced to flee over a confrontation with his aristocratic schoolmates, he becomes a kitchen boy in a castle and falls in love with the count's daughter. His musical talents attract the attention of the count and his daughter, Angeline. The count promotes him to a higher servant rank, and Angeline begins to test his seemingly unrequited love, finally giving him a golden thread for safekeeping which Lionel sews under his skin. When later she asks about it, he cuts it out of his chest and thereby wins her uncompromising devotion. This "golden thread"—a clever symbol of the precious bond which henceforth ties their hearts together—gives the novel its name. The discovery of their secret love causes Lionel to flee the count's wrath. But after many dangerous adventures, hardships, and tribulations, the lovers are reunited. The brave and resourceful Lionel has escaped the ambush of his assassins with the aid of his faithful lion; he has performed extraordinary services in battle and was knighted by the grateful king. The count now consents to the marriage, and Lionel eventually becomes his successor as regent of the shire.

Jörg Wickram drew on several literary traditions and proved himself an astute assimilator in the process. His sources include the folk and fairy tale, myth and biblical lore, picaresque and humanistic writing, and medieval romance—particularly as mediated through the popular prose adaptations of the chapbook (*Volksbuch*). The fairy-tale tone of the novel's introductory sentence, with its evocation of indefinite time and distant, yet specific, place (Portugal), prepares the reader for a story of simultaneously universal and historical significance. Dark forests, ghosts, and helping animals are additional fairy-tale motifs. The moral underpinnings are provided by the Bible. Lionel's initially low station and the craftiness and tenacity guiding his will to succeed parallel the contemporaneous picaresque novel. And Wickram's pedagogical fervor, his moral *engagement* and tenacious commitment to the education of the lower classes, shares the didactic concerns of the humanists, although without the satirical acerbity fashionable at the time.

The adopted ideas and motifs often serve multiple functions. Thus the linkage of our protagonist with the lion—recalling among other sources the *Iwein* romance, Christian legends, and various chapbook episodes—not only facilitates the symbolic attribution of the lion's "princely virtues" as heraldic symbols of noble strength and courage to Lionel's essential character but also signifies his "chosen" status in a notable variation on the medieval belief in preordained social rank, for the animal seeks out Lionel's family even before the baby's birth, often resting its head in the pregnant mother's lap. Its harmonious rapport with the human world in a nearly pastoral setting evokes parallels to the peaceable kingdom. Yet the tame lion is also perceived as a public sensation, a veritable tourist attraction to visitors from near and far—thus revealing a more realistic treatment of the originally miraculous motif. Even if the Lionel-lion linkage is read largely as a concession making the hero's meteoric rise from kitchen boy to count more palatable to the aristocrats among his readers, it does not diminish Wickram's artistic skill in adapting the fantastic material to his progressive social message.

The whole adventurous typology of chivalric romance, with its stock repertory of dangerous encounters, disguises, and intrigues, of mistaken identities and intercepted love letters, of hermits, messengers, and rogues, informs the rich narrative action. Much as the courtly knight proved his valor in adventure, Lionel triumphs over adversity, fighting outlaws in the forest, rescuing the innocent, and punishing the guilty.

His virtuous demeanor echoes codes of idealized courtly conduct, albeit with a shifting view toward a new social ethic: the chivalrous concept of "triuwe," for example, the social bond connecting lord and vassal in reciprocal loyalty, has been replaced by fervent friendship among commoners and across class boundaries; the principle of "arebeit" resurfaces in Lionel's assiduous industry; and chivalrous beneficence reappears in the charitable conduct of Lionel's natural and adopted family, as the poor share their children and the rich share their wealth in Christian accord. Striving for personal excellence becomes a moral imperative for the middle-class protagonist as it had been for the chivalrous knight. Like the great medieval poets, Wickram follows his personal vision of a rapprochement of the individual and society, of spiritual and secular values.

While Wickram's *Golden Thread* may not rival Gottfried's *Tristan* in formal and intellectual sophistication, its artistic achievements are considerable when measured against the "Volksbuch" and still cruder "Schwank"—the dominant prose literature of the time. Even compared to his own *Rollwagenbüchlein*, the novel operates on a more elevated level of discourse, with sensuous descriptive language, metaphorical devices and other rhetorical embellishments, and careful avoidance of vulgarisms. Instead of a rambling string of discrete actions and figural stereotypes, Wickram has reduced his material to a manageable sequence of skillfully connected episodes and a limited number of well-developed characters drawn with sympathy and understanding. The love relationship between Angeline and Lionel is patiently constructed in measured increments of interest and intensity on its obstacle course of repeated testing and confirmation, of separation, hardships, and intrigue—its steady and insistent growth rendering believable the ultimate power of love to transcend the barriers of social station. Interspersed songs and sporadic monologues reveal the inner workings of the soul. And the psychological motivation even of supporting characters can be subtle and complex, as, for example, in the case of the count's conflicting values: torn between the principle of social honor and the impulse of filial love, and further aggravated by guilt over his earlier assassination plan against Lionel and fear of its discovery, the count is hardly a rigid embodiment of an unbending ruling type but is rather a troubled human being deliberating difficult choices, changing his mind, and ready to compromise in the interest of communal concord.

Wickram's artistic reluctance to stereotype also throws light on his ideological position. He was no raving revolutionary. Though his sympathies clearly lie with the lower classes, he refuses to paint a one-dimensional portrait of the "evil" nobility. He rejects the notion of noble birth as the chief determinant of opportunity and stature but will not advocate a transfer of social prerogatives from one class to another. The privilege of higher rank must be earned. The aristocrats must prove they are worthy of it; and the lower classes may ascend to it through diligence, intelligence, and substantive achievement—as the persevering, God-fearing Lionel had shown. An eloquent extoller of emerging bourgeois values and virtues, Wickram ultimately seemed more interested in demonstrating the productive social and moral potential of the rising middle class than in radical criticism of the feudal establishment.

Lionel's success story, his remarkable social climb from shepherd's son to ruling nobility, reflects, to be sure, the rising aspirations of the lower classes for upward social mobility. But his exemplary journey from birth to maturity also provides an early prototype of the German "Entwicklungsroman"—a novel of education or development which minutely maps the hero's spiritual and physical progress toward the fulfillment of his destiny. Grimmelshausen's *Simplicissimus* of 1669 would take the next step in building a venerable tradition in this genre, which crested with Goethe's *Wilhelm Meister* and the Romantics around the turn of the nineteenth century.

Literary historians have recognized Jörg Wickram as one of the most significant pioneers of German prose fiction, if not the father of the German novel. He was an acute observer of the socio-historical realities of his time, and, in spite of strong idealizing tendencies prompted by his pedagogical ethos, he also made his mark as a pioneer of realism in German literature. A member of the emerging middle class himself, he became one of its most eloquent advocates in the cause of social and political advancement. What makes Wickram particularly attractive to the modern reader is his ability to combine historical consciousness with social commitment and artistic innovation without sacrificing the entertainment value of his narrative talents.

Jörg Wickram had no immediate successors of comparable stature. Broad public taste reverted to the potboiling chivalrous adventures and love stories in the mold of the "Amadis" novel. It was not until over a century later that *The Golden Thread* found a worthy successor in Grimmelshausens's work.

Ronald Salter

Tufts University
Medford, Massachusetts

TRANSLATOR'S NOTE

The Golden Thread is the first English translation of Jörg Wickram's 1557 prose work, *Der Goldfaden*. The basis of this translation is the 1968 edition of *Der Goldtfaden* by Hans-Gert Roloff. Roloff has kept the text of the 1557 edition without editing it, leaving spelling and punctuation in the original form.

The woodcuts have been taken from Rütten & Loening's 1963 reedition of Clemens Brentano's adaptation of *Der Goldfaden* into modern German. As in the case of most early works, the artwork was most likely done by an anonymous employee of Jakob Froelich in Strassburg. Actually, the plates seem to be composed of generic half plates, which can be recombined in different configurations elsewhere.

Basically a translation is an adaptation of a text from one language, or from one period, to another. The translation here is an adaptation of a sixteenth-century German text into modern English. Hence, the translator tries to mediate between two languages as well as two periods.

Besides the usual challenges encountered when rendering German texts into English (long sentences, genders, stylistic devices specific to the German language, and so on) and those difficulties peculiar to this text, there was one additional problem: rendering and maintaining the tone of *Der Goldfaden*. In trying to retain the flavor of the older text, the translator chose to use mainly modern English with a few slightly archaic words akin to fairy-tale vocabulary. While being easily understood, such a style still gives the feeling of quaintness and remoteness in time. In the nineteenth century Clemens Brentano had already modernized *Der Goldfaden* in a similar way.

Although Wickram uses the German of the sixteenth century, vocabulary and sentence structure are similar to those of the dialects spoken in Alsace today. These dialects have not significantly evolved since Wickram's time, for at the time when high German was being elaborated, Alsace had essentially become part of France. Being of Alsatian origin, the translator has drawn upon his linguistic expertise to render *Der Goldfaden* into *The Golden Thread*.

A first glance at the original may be disturbing to a modern reader used to standard punctuation, since Wickram uses only three signs of punctuation: the period, the parenthesis and the slant (/). The period occurs mainly at the ends of paragraphs; parentheses are used only when an English writer would use commas to indicate parenthetical matter and have been replaced by commas. The slant is *The Golden Thread*'s standard punctuation and ends the great majority of sentences. These signs have been modernized and standardized.

A few other modernizations have been made to Wickram's text. These are mostly stylistic adaptations and are indicated below.

Wickram's style has an epic flavor, relying heavily on repetition, a device which was current in Wickram's time. One of Wickram's favorite words is the intensive *gar* (quite, very, indeed, thoroughly). Another is *Fleiss* (diligence), which comes directly from Wickram's middle-class consciousness and serves to remind the reader of the didactic intent of the author. Since modern readers have little use for such repetitions—which rapidly become boring—they have been avoided whenever possible or practical. Also Wickram seems to have great affection for words such as "above-mentioned" and "aforesaid" (a bleed-over from his career as town clerk?). These have also been left out.

Often, Wickram uses a combination of two synonyms (for example, "fear and fright"). Since the second of such a pair adds little to the text where meaning is concerned, this stylistic device of Wickram's has been left out of this translation, especially since such repetitions do not occur regularly. At times Wickram uses a given word several times in rapid sequence (e.g., cheerful or friendly). Whenever possible, such repetitions have also been eliminated.

At the end of several chapters, Wickram uses a little formula best rendered as "and thus did things remain." Since they do not add significantly to the flow of the story, these codae were left out of the translation.

Being Protestant and coming in the immediate wake of the Reformation (Luther was only about twenty years his senior), our author must have been an avid Bible reader, for he often uses biblical expressions. Corresponding English expressions have been used.

As one of the local Meistersinger, Wickram introduces into his narration songs which have been rendered in meaning only, the rhymes being too difficult to adapt without having to betray the original meaning.

Proper names have been given close equivalents in English. Thus, for example, Hermann becomes Herman, Florina becomes Florence, and so on. Lewfried, the protagonist, has been adapted to Lionel, a name which, like the original, speaks of a leonine disposition. At times, Wickram (or his typesetter) was not careful about keeping the names of the women straight. As Brentano has done in his reedition of *The Golden Thread*, these names were changed to conform to the story line (for example, in chapter 2 one of the characters is named Laureta in the chapter head and Lyseta throughout the rest of the chapter). In a similar fashion, the translator changed geographic names whenever necessary, since Wickram seems to become confused about his hero's exact whereabouts (Merida and Salamanca are thus mixed up). Also, toward the end of the story, Castile changes from victim to villain in the original.

Occasionally Wickram shows a sense of humor by inserting puns and word plays into his text. Such puns are untranslatable into English and are usually given a straight translation. For instance, one time that Angeline wants to be left alone by her maidens, she claims to be unwell. She dismisses her maidens, expressing the hope that her "Sachen" will be better the next day. An obvious meaning is that she will be in a better mood the next day, but in the Alsatian dialect the word "Sachen" designates also a woman's menstruation. None of these puns or word plays, however, significantly affects the meaning of the text.

All in all, the translator has endeavored to present *The Golden Thread* in the way Wickram had written it, had he lived today. The task has not always been an easy one, and at times the translator had to distance himself from the original in order not to follow it too laboriously. The result, though, should be a pleasant story to read as well as a contribution to the scholarly world.

Pierre Kaufke

Pensacola, Florida

THE GOLDEN THREAD
(1557)

CHAPTER I

How the Herdsman Erik Was Keeping His Herd, and How a Huge Lion Came Daily among His Herd without Harming It, Even Helped Keep It like a Tame Dog.

Many years ago there lived in the kingdom of Portugal a poor man named Erik. Though he was very poor, God had blessed him with many children, both sons and daughters. God had also granted these children such wondrous beauty that neither toil, fear, nor poverty could sadden Erik in the least. For as soon as he came home at night, he would lay aside pick and hoe, gather around him his young and beautiful children, and frolic with them as merrily as if he had not spent the whole day working hard. However, as soon as his children grew a little older, rich merchants would adopt them and rear them diligently and well. And when finally they would reach maturity, they were provided for and endowed honorably.

Nobody, however, saw fit to come to Erik's aid and assistance until his wife Felicia—for this was her name—bore her last son. With this child, good fortune and happiness aplenty befell her and her husband on this earth.

The good, pious, and loyal Erik, had agreed to keep his community's cattle so as to better earn his livelihood. While he held this office, a rare and unheard of marvel came to pass. Once when he was grazing his cattle, his wife Felicia brought him his breakfast to the pastures. They sat together under a shady tree to escape the heat of the sun and cheerfully ate the food which God had provided for them. While they were thus sitting there, both his dogs began to bark most fearfully, and the cattle huddled together with great snorting. A good herdsman, Erik grasped his staff and ran to his herd in all haste. In the midst of it there was a grim and mighty lion, the sight of which frightened him no little. The lion, however, gazed at him very kindly and welcomed him with a meek countenance, beating his tail against the ground as does a dog at the call of its master.

Erik marveled greatly at this sight and was still at a loss as to what to do when the lion withdrew quite peacefully and without harming the cattle in any way. Erik, the good herdsman, returned to Felicia, his wife, who was still waiting for him under the tree. When she saw him so pale and so completely bereft of all human color, she feared exceedingly and arose immediately, crying, "Oh, Erik, my beloved husband, why is your face so white all of a sudden? Oh, for the love of God, tell me what frightened you so!"

The herdsman comforted his beloved wife as best he could and told her everything that had occurred with the lion, at which the good woman marveled greatly. Then they sat down again to finish their meal as well as they could. Since noon had come and gone, good Felicia left to return home. She had not gone very far when she encountered the same lion, which frightened her considerably. The lion, however, behaved quite as harmlessly and peacefully as it had earlier toward Erik, the shepherd. Nonetheless, she ran back to her husband and told him of meeting the lion. So Erik kept her with him until the evening, for he worried lest his wife take fright and suffer harm therefrom, as she was heavy with child.

When the sun went down, he drove his cattle home and told the story of what had happened to some of his neighbors who took it for a joke and not the truth. But the good man did not wish to argue with them; therefore, he let it go at that and remained silent about the matter ever afterwards. His wife, however, refused to return to the pastures, for she had been so frightened that she worried lest it hurt the seed she bore beneath her heart. No less did her husband Erik worry, for he knew full well that his wife's time was nigh; therefore, he daily prayed to God most earnestly that He grant his wife a happy delivery.

Before long, word of the lion spread far and wide, for the beast came daily and went about among Erik's cattle no differently from dogs brought up with livestock from their earliest age. In the same manner would the lion keep the cattle. And when evening came, he would return to the forest harmlessly and with stately tread. Word reached the king who forbade anyone in his entire kingdom to inflict harm on the lion under pain of losing his favor. Thus, rich burghers and merchants—and there were many indeed—came from far and wide to see this lion which was to be found daily with the herdsman.

When finally the tameness of the lion had become well established, people came daily, bringing him meat and other food so that he was fed quite well. Finally, after the animal had been shown such friendliness, he became so tame that at night he would follow Erik home and lie in front of his house with his dogs as if wanting to help guard it. In the morning, he would go back to the pasture with Erik and his cattle. This went on until Erik's wife, who was by now very close to giving birth, no longer feared the lion.

There happened to be in the city an extremely wealthy merchant who had but one child whom his wife had recently borne him after having been barren for over twelve years. Moreover, during childbirth, a mishap had befallen her and they had been greatly concerned for her life. She had been told with no uncertainty that she would never again be able to bear a child. Every day this merchant would come with food for the lion so that he might fully satisfy his curiosity about this marvel.

One day it so happened that he found Felicia in the pasture with her husband. She was sitting with the lion, his head resting in her lap. The merchant marveled greatly at the sight, especially when he saw that the woman who was sitting there was with child. The lion was quick to recognize the merchant who oftentimes had brought him food and showed him great friendliness. Herman, for this was the name of the merchant, went to Erik and questioned him fully on all things: for how long the lion had been seeking his company and also for how long his wife had been with child. In all this the herdsman informed him thoroughly with short and simple words.

"My dear Erik," said Herman then, "should it come to pass that God grant you an offspring, I beg you not to disdain me, but to accept me as godfather for your child. In exchange, I promise you to raise the child like my own flesh and blood, and to provide it the same love, care, and education, as well as clothing, food, and drink as my own lawful son. Should then God prolong its days and let it reach maturity, I shall bestow upon it a liberal dowry, whether it be a son or a daughter. In addition to all this, I shall also provide for you and your wife in such a way that both of you may earn your living with less exertion than heretofore." This promise and comfort, Erik accepted with great joy and gratitude. Thereupon Herman blessed them and rode back to the city to inform his wife of all these things. She concurred joyfully, eagerly looking forward to those times.

CHAPTER II
❦ *How Felicia Was Delivered of a Son in the Presence of Laureta, the Merchant's Wife; What Further Came to Pass with the Lion.*

After her days were accomplished and Felicia, the herdsman's wife, had carried to its term the seed which God had granted her, she went into labor. As Herman had ordered it, she immediately sent her husband to her future patroness in the city. The merchant immediately boarded a spring carriage with his wife and other good friends and set out for Erik's village. They had not been there for very long when matters became quite serious with good Felicia. And thus, in the presence of Laureta and other modest women, she brought into the world a fine son. As soon as Laureta perceived this, she ran to her husband Herman, requesting of him rich reward for those good tidings. He rejoiced exceedingly when he learned that Felicia had been delivered of a son.

Now when the child was being bathed, a birthmark in the form of a lion's paw was found on the left side of its chest, toward the heart. As soon as Herman and his company noticed it, they all cried out together that certainly this child would grow to be a brave and manly hero, because of this and other signs that were discovered on its body.

An industrious and prudent woman, Laureta saw to it that poor Felicia was supplied not only with everything she needed for a quick recovery of her strength, but also with costly bed linens, blankets, and cushions as rich as those of the wives of the richest burghers. Then Laureta ordered the child carried to the baptismal font. But when the infant was carried out of the house, the lion began to roar as dreadfully and threateningly as if someone were attempting to steal his own cub.

When the merchant saw all of these things, he deliberated with his good friends. Since the lion had lived so long with the shepherd in such a peaceful and friendly manner, they decided to name the infant Lionel. The baby was carried to and from baptism amidst great joy. Then Herman invited many people from the village, men and women, to the inn for a sumptuous meal.

True to his promise, Herman entrusted the shepherd Erik with the tenancy of a farm. As for the infant, he commended it to the good care of its rightful mother until it should be at least one year old. In addition, he sent her wholesome food and drink. As soon as she had reached the fourth week after her delivery, Erik gave up his staff and betook himself to his new tenancy, which lay close to the city. He took along his lion, which became friendlier as time went on, for whenever Erik went to the city on business, the lion accompanied him and was fed by everyone.

Finally the king of the land heard so much about the lion that he had him brought to his royal court, at which Erik was so sorely grieved that he was as downcast as if one of his blood relatives had departed in death. Felicia and Herman sorrowed no less.

Lionel, the infant, was fed at his mother's breast and fed well, so that after a few days the baby was handsome and lively, for his mother was well provided for by Herman and his wife. In exchange, they tended what belonged to their master with great care and thrift, so that in a short time, he came to notice that his farm was well-stocked, for God looked with favor upon these two, especially since they were godfearing, pious, and righteous and were not tempted to rob their master. Unfortunately, there are not many such tenants nowadays. There are many, however, who after three or four seasons, leave their properties unmanured and suck them bone-dry, returning them exhausted to the hands of their landlords.

CHAPTER III

How Lionel Was Taken Away from His Mother, Brought to His Godfather in the City and Reared with Great Kindness.

When the merchant had reason to believe that his adopted son had sufficiently enjoyed the milk of his mother—for now he was more than a year old—he sent for Erik and his wife, requesting also that they bring along their son.

Both of them arrived with the child on a Sunday morning. Herman had had a lavish meal prepared, to which he had invited all his good friends. Now when everyone was seated, he addressed them, saying: "My dearest and best friends, none of you should be able to say, or even to think, that I gave my promise and my word under the influence of wine or of a sleeping potion; therefore, I beg you all to listen to me and to be true witnesses to my pledge and my promise, for I discussed this matter with my spouse Laureta and decided with her consent to treat this baby boy here no differently than my own son whom she bore me; I will do so today and ever afterwards. However, this should be no reason for him to deny his parents. Therefore, none of my household will let him forget who are his real father and mother. At all times, moreover, these will have free access to their son, whom I shall bring up with everything he needs until he reaches maturity. Then I shall provide him with an honest girl and endow him like my one and only son. I have invited you to this meal to witness all this. Therefore, make merry with me." Since this pledge and promise were well to the liking of the guests, and since food and drink were served anon, the meal proceeded amidst great merriment.

Afterwards, Herman took the child and ordered his wife Laureta to take good care of him, which she did according to her husband's request. The shepherd Erik and his wife, however, left the city in great sorrow, for their parental feelings were stirred. But since they were able to behold their son every day as they visited the house of the merchant, they soon forgot their sorrow.

When Lionel and the merchant's son reached the age of understanding, Herman sent them to school where, after a short time, they were studying diligently and well, so that everyone, young and old, wondered at their application; especially did they wonder at Lionel, whose intelligence and quick wit were those of one twenty years his senior. Their fellow pupils gained such regard for him that they unanimously established him as their king and ruler.

After he had been chosen their king, Lionel gave each boy an office according to his merits. And after he had organized his affairs and his realm most efficiently, all of the young pupils had even greater regard for him.

In their city of Salamanca there was another school that was attended by far more boys of noble origin than Lionel's. These banded together and held the other school in contempt, together with its king, for he was a herdsman's son, and not one of the nobility. This scorn deeply hurt the feelings of the other boys. They brought it to the attention of their king, who exhorted his followers to seek revenge, which they all promised to do.

In Lionel's school there was also a young boy of noble birth who would tell and report to the adverse party everything intended against them. Very soon they established a king of their own, a proud and arrogant young nobleman. Almost at once, and without the knowledge of their schoolmasters, the two schools declared war and appointed a place where they might meet in battle. Lionel was well satisfied with this. He and his companions made ready as best as they could, so that they might defeat their enemies.

CHAPTER IV
🍐 *How Lionel Prepared Himself; How His Companions Fashioned Armor from Tree Bark, and How He Was Reported to the Headmaster for Having a Boy Chastised and Beaten with Switches.*

Lionel called a meeting of all his subjects and exhorted them to set about their preparations resolutely, so that they might be better equipped and protected than their enemies. Each of them was to fashion a backplate and breastplate out of bark stripped off trees. They all followed these directions and secretly looked for bark out of which to make brassards, breastplates, and backplates, so as to be reasonably well protected from thrusts and blows.

The treacherous young nobleman, however, took note of everything and, as soon as the opportunity arose, reported it to the other king, who equipped himself with the same kind of armor and protection. On the appointed Sunday, they met at the specified place. A cautious youth, Lionel commanded his troops in person. He established his advantage at once by occupying a hilltop, and there he awaited his enemies. While both sides were still taking up their positions, Lionel asked to parley with the other king, his opponent, who accepted readily. Thus, they agreed that they would use neither harmful weapons made of iron or steel, nor clubs or pointed sticks, but only wooden swords. Also, no rock was to be thrown by either side; everyone, however, was allowed to throw wet clay or soft earth.

Then, both sides joined battle. Several times the boys of the rival king attempted to dislodge Lionel from his vantage point, but to no avail whatsoever. The companies of the latter occupied the top of the hill and pelted their foes heavily with clods of earth while their comrades at the foot of the hill, armed with wooden swords, mightily withstood their advance. Finally Lionel's opponents grew so weak and weary that they were unable either to throw or strike. As soon as they gave up and fled from the hill, Lionel engaged in pursuit with his companions.

Their opponents acknowledged defeat and begged for mercy. Their king, whom Lionel had captured, sued for peace. He also told of the boy who had betrayed the secrets. Lionel had him brought before him and severely beaten with switches. The boy felt so humiliated that he complained to his mother who took the matter to his father. This one became so angry with Lionel that he reported him to the headmaster, telling him that if he, the headmaster, would not punish Lionel, he would do so himself. The headmaster complied with his request, and, to show his goodwill, proposed to send for Lionel and punish him at once.

One of Lionel's companions overheard them and rushed to warn him. Upon hearing this, the poor king was dreadfully frightened. He was also at a loss as to what to do. At that time, he was not quite twelve years old. Nevertheless, he did not give it much thought but went straight home. He betook himself to his room and wrote the following letter:

> "Although you have been very kind to me, dearest godfather, and still are so daily to my father and mother, I have to part from you. My companions and fellow pupils elected me as their king, and now I am about to be chastised by my headmaster and a nobleman whose son I ordered punished. Oh, I would have been all too ashamed to face my adversaries whom I have so valiantly overcome with my companions! My opponent would be full of glee if he should learn that I—who was the king of my companions—have been whipped so foully and dispossessed of my kingdom!
>
> "Therefore, dear lord and father, I beg you to forgive me in the name of God. In exchange, I promise you never to forget your good and fatherly advice as long as God will grant me life; I will follow this advice at all times and direct my life accordingly. I beg you also to remain committed to my poor father and mother and not to let them suffer because of my folly. As for me, I shall depart. May God bless you and all of yours with everlasting health."

Having written this letter and sealed it with wax, Lionel went to supper very sadly, a fact which Herman noticed immediately. As he asked him what was amiss, Lionel answered with a very feeble and sad voice that nothing was amiss with him, but that he would like to visit his family. His godfather readily granted him permission.

Lionel, however, had no mind to go to his father and mother, but only said so not to arouse his godfather's suspicion. He gave the matter little thought after he had been granted permission, but he put on his worst clothes and went his way after placing the letter in his school bag. He set out with no intention of ever returning.

CHAPTER V
🍎 How Lionel Found His Way to the Kitchen at a Count's Court and Became a Kitchen Apprentice; Also, How the Master Cook Took a Liking to Him, and Further of His Nice Singing.

Lionel set out in great sorrow. He knew quite well that his father and mother would look for him with much grief—as, in fact, they did. His godfather, the merchant, was also sore at heart about the boy, especially when he discovered in his school bag the letter which took away all hope that the boy would ever return. His classmates mourned no less for their king.

Lionel journeyed until he had completely spent what cash he had acquired in better times. By now he was so far from his country that he had high hopes that no one would be able to recognize him. He came to a beautiful city in which there was a mighty castle where a count held court. "If only fortune were kind enough to let me enter that castle," he told himself, "I would behave in such a diligent manner that in no time I would become a horse-guard." And with such thoughts, he headed for the castle gate. He knocked and asked the gatekeeper if there were any need for a young lad in the castle. The gatekeeper gave him a favorable reply and told him to wait, that he would go and announce him to the master cook, for a kitchen apprentice had just run away. Before long he came back with the cook who said, as soon as he caught sight of Lionel, "I am afraid that you are too young, my boy; otherwise, I would give you a chance!"

"Dear master," answered Lionel, "do not let my young age and my small size fool you. I shall prove capable of carrying out your orders as valiantly as one twice my size." The cook marveled at the clever speech of the youth, took him by the hand and led him to the kitchen. There, Lionel behaved very valiantly indeed! He carried out everything his master entrusted to his hands as skillfully as if he had done nothing else in his entire life. He also sang so heartily and so happily that he made time pass quickly for all those around him. His master came to like and value the boy who was obliging to the whole household.

In the summer months, once he had discharged his chores after the evening meal, he would sing in a high voice in a nice garden behind the castle, and then the whole household would lend an eager ear to his singing, for young Lionel had a most sweet and lovely voice.

As it happened, the count had a beautiful daughter named Angeline. With her there lived many beautiful maidens who had been entrusted to her care, for she was a paragon of good manners and etiquette in which her late mother had instructed her full well. She excelled in all artistic crafts such as embroidering, knitting, weaving, sewing, and anything that could be fashioned of silver and gold. She must have surpassed and excelled even Arachne who outwove Pallas. With song or strings—especially with lute and harp—she would have been second not even to Sappho herself. She was also kind to everyone and gentle toward the whole household.

Since all the windows of her apartments opened onto the garden at the back of the castle, Angeline and her damsels enjoyed no little the happy singing of the youth. The count, however, could not hear him from his apartments.

This lasted all summer long, until autumn was over and the dull cold days arrived with their heavy, leaden clouds. Then Lionel was heard no more in the garden. In wintertime, when making merry in the halls of the castle, the retainers of the count would often entice Lionel to let them hear his voice, at which his master, the cook, was always particularly pleased. In this manner, Lionel came into close contact with the retainers of the court and became acquainted with many and diverse ballads of chivalry. In the course of that winter, he also began composing his own artful lyrics and songs, an activity which was his only ambition beyond his occupation.

The household came to like him so well that everyone wanted to be around him, and he was given so many nice gifts by the retainers of the court that in a short time he was well off. Whenever he was presented with anything made of gold or silver, he entrusted it to his master, and whenever he had gathered enough, had nice clothes made for himself so that he always had smart and well-tailored clothes to wear in addition to his court uniform.

CHAPTER VI
How, According to Her Custom, Angeline, the Count's Daughter, Gave a New Year's Present to All the Retainers of the Court; How She Forgot Only Lionel, the Kitchen Apprentice, Who Was Sorely Grieved.

That same winter, with the coming of the New Year, Lady Angeline handed out New Year presents to all the members of the household according to degree of nobility or office. Even the least of the stable boys received some nice handkerchief or scarf, after which they gathered to show off what had been bestowed upon them.

As it happened, Lionel was also present, and everyone asked to see his New Year present, too. Lionel, however, had not received anything, and thus he had nothing to show. And yet, he was not downcast, for he thought, "Who knows, Lady Angeline may not know me; but I shall betake myself into her sight. Who knows but in her mercy she might still recognize me." So Lionel betook himself often and diligently to paths and ways where he thought Lady Angeline might pass, but it was all in vain, for she did not notice him at all, which profoundly distressed him. Furthermore, Cupid had so wounded him with his arrow that he was inflamed with a great and passionate love for the Lady Angeline. So ardently did the flame of love consume him that neither day, hour, nor even a single moment went by in which he would not think of her beauty.

One Sunday when he had discharged quite early the chores his master had bid him to do, the whole household gathered in the great hall of the castle, for it was cruelly cold outside. When they looked about and saw the master cook and his aide but not Lionel, they all wondered and asked the cook about him. "I don't know where he is," he said. "He left the kitchen as soon as he was finished with his chores; perhaps he went to the city on some business."

But matters stood quite differently with Lionel. Greatly dejected, he was sitting in the garden, hidden from sight, for he did not want to share his secret with anyone. Complaining to himself about his grief and sorrow, he began to talk to himself about the fickleness and inconsistency of fortune.

"Oh fortune," he was saying, "how fickle you are! In my childhood you took me out of my father's poor thatched hut where I would have fared so well! Had I not enjoyed fine and sweet days, I would now be working for my father or some other herdsman who would provide me with food and clothing! I would be happy to drink the water of fresh, clear springs, as well as the thick, sweet milk of goats and cows. I would drive out my cows at noon, and when the sun would be about to set, I would drive them home again and pass the time until the evening meal in a warm room or by the fireside. In the morning, it would be but little effort and work for me to go to the woods, gather a load of dry wood and bring it home to cook breakfast.

"And in summertime, I would fare better yet; I can say with good reason that at the beginning of spring no folks of any estate have more fun, joy, pleasure, and delight than the herdsmen in the fields. They behold the wonders of God, how the leafless trees, which in winter look as if they were dead, bud out amidst sweet fragrance and dainty blossoms. And what should I say of the lovely song of the birds! They harmonize with quivering voices and best each other in song! The merry sight of the many-colored little flowers with their innumerable shapes gives the beholder no little delight, rapture, and joy.

"Of all these things, I, poor Lionel, must be bereft! And only you, Fortune, can I blame for it, since you did not wish me to stay with my godfather and provider. Ah! Why did you take me out of my godfather's house? Why did you begrudge my being educated so liberally and so well! Moreover, you willed me to become king and to rule over my fellows, and that rule was the cause of all the afflictions in which I am now hopelessly caught up and entangled. Alas! Poor afflicted lad that I am, who is there in this world to comfort me now that I am inflamed with such a great love for the one who has ignored me, who despises me, and for whom it will never be possible to speak a single kind word to me in my whole life? For if she did, I would wish nothing else than to live and die in her service. But why would she need me? I am a poor herdsman's son, born of the lowest estate, and she, with so many knights, counts, barons, and noblemen at her service, she can find enough who would serve her with pleasure."

Thus, the good youth went on complaining to himself most sorely until he could no longer stay in the garden because of the frost. Moreover, it was time for him to go about his chores in the kitchen. He left the garden and went to work quite out of sorts. When asked where he had been, he replied that he had gone to the city to look at the merry dwellings of the burghers.

CHAPTER VII
❦ *How One Day the Count Discovered Lionel in the Garden, Singing in a Most Lovely Manner under a Rose Tree, and How the Count Removed Him from the Kitchen.*

When winter was over and sweet and lovely May had refreshed all the pastures and clad them with dainty flowers, Lionel resumed his old activity during his leisure time, for he had somewhat cooled the fire of love by avoiding all the places where he could imagine meeting Lady Angeline. One day perchance, and without worrying that anyone would come into the garden at such a time, he was singing with a voice so clear and lovely that the birds could not help answering him with their own song.

The count was strolling in that same garden with some foreign visitors. He hardly knew the youth whom he had never noticed before and whose voice he had never heard. The foreign visitors who had come into the garden with him thought that the count had provided special entertainment for them. But since the count marveled no less at the lovely singing, they wondered no little when he arose without a word and remained silent until Lionel had finished a song. Then he said: "That is certainly a wondrous bird in my garden; I have never been aware of it before!"

With these words, he stepped to the rose arbor and caught sight of young Lionel sitting under it, singing cheerfully. The count and the other gentlemen stood still outside the arbor until Lionel had completed his song, and then they joined him. Lionel feared exceedingly when he gazed upon his master, the count; so frightened was he that he could not stand up. The count and the other gentlemen were well aware of it. "Cheer up, young man," the count addressed him gently, "this discovery will be a very lucky one for you, for I can clearly see by your livery that you belong to my household, although I do not know in what capacity. Therefore, you must not withhold anything from me but tell me your station; if it is too low, I shall see to it that it be improved."

Thus, Lionel told him everything, upon which the count said: "You should be able to enjoy your voice and your good singing and have another and better office than you have now. So from now on, you shall be page to my daughter Angeline. There you will fare better than in the kitchen."

The count took him by the hand and led him to his daughter. As soon as Lionel caught sight of Lady Angeline, the flame of love was kindled anew within him, and much more ardently did it burn than ever before. But he was able to keep it completely concealed and was filled with joy at entering her service.

"Angeline, my dear daughter," said the count, "it is no secret to me that you need a well-mannered boy in your apartments; this is why I have brought you this lad that you might use him as you wish in your service, for this is the only duty he is to perform." Thus, the count spoke to his daughter.

Lionel was a very well-mannered as well as an extremely handsome youth. Of this the maiden had already taken notice and, therefore, kindly thanked her father with modest words for supplying her quite so paternally with everything she needed.

When the count took leave of his daughter, he took Lionel

with him. The lad was full of joy; he went to his master, the cook, and informed him of the course of his fortune. Although the latter did not like to lose him in the kitchen, he did not begrudge him in the least having such a gracious lord in the person of the count, and he exhorted Lionel always to perform his duties with utmost diligence so that in due time he might accede to a still higher and better office. Lionel promised to do so, thanked him for the kindness he had shown him while he worked under him, and left for his new office and station, where he started out as deftly as if he had spent his whole life in the lady's apartment at a count's court.

Lady Angeline, in the meantime, had found out that Lionel was the very youth who was singing in the garden. Therefore, she was particularly pleased that Lionel was to enter her service. Her maidens rejoiced no less, for they hoped that from time to time Lionel would entertain and amuse them with his singing.

CHAPTER VIII

How Angeline Asked Lionel for a Song, and How He Composed a Complaint about His Wretchedness; How It Impressed Angeline.

Since Lionel behaved so valiantly and well in her service, Lady Angeline came to like him well, and when she had grown somewhat used to him, she addressed him one day by saying: "Lionel, my maidens inform me that your singing is beyond compare; therefore, I would like to hear one of your songs, and I entreat you to let me hear your voice."

Lionel, then, stood before his lady, blushing deeply with embarrassment. He answered her modestly: "Noble and gracious lady, even if I had to accomplish things far more strenuous and difficult to please your grace, I would do so gladly."

And thus, he struck up a lovely song which he had composed himself and in which he heartily bemoaned his wretchedness, giving special mention to the fact that Angeline had not given him anything for the New Year. None of the maidens grasped the meaning of the song, except Angeline, who remembered only now how she had bestowed gifts upon the whole household but had forgotten only Lionel. Nevertheless, she was not quite sure of exactly what he meant by it. Therefore, she often asked him to sing the song of his wretchedness which ran as follows:

(To the tune of "Gang mir aus den Bohnen"*)

Wretchedness! Unbearable yoke!
You are so despicable
That no one wants your company
After considering well
How completely worthless
You are on this earth.
One shudders at your thought!
No matter
How hard you try
No one wants your company.

Wretchedness! Unbearable yoke
You weight me down so much!
You will find no one on this earth
To be your friend.
If you enter a house
There you stay,
And never again will happiness
Dwell therein
Nor wealth abound.
At such time all hope's in vain!

That's what was my lot last New Year!
I suffered because of you.
As least of the household,
I received nothing.
That is why I don't like you,
For day and night
I was despised
By all the other servants.

---

*Wilhelm Bondzio believes that the songs Wickram introduces into his narratives are adapted from popular melodies. In this case, the song would be a very popular one in the mid-sixteenth century; its refrain began by "Nun gang mir aus den Bohnen," "now get out of my beans" ("Nachwort" in Jörg Wickram, *Der Goldfaden*, ed. Wilhelm Bondzio. Berlin: Rütten & Loening, 1963, p. 286).

Every one of them
Received some gift.
That's why I hate you so.

Lady Angeline listened to this song very intently and was convinced at once that it had been composed on her behalf. However, she did not ask any questions about it but let matters rest there. Henceforth, however, she took great pains not to bestow upon Lionel any gift or present, for she had already devised a secret plan. Nevertheless, she showed herself no less gracious and kind toward him, asking him often to sing for her, and also, from time to time, she reminded him of that particular song, which he was always willing to perform. All told, it was not too much for him, for this was his way to serve the maiden, which he did with all his might. Angeline was well aware of his application.

When autumn with its cold winds had bared the tall trees of their leaves, winter set in with brutal force; fields and meadows were covered with snow, and presently the New Year arrived. This was the time Angeline had chosen to carry out her plan. She provided herself with many and sundry fair presents for the whole household, but she prepared nothing for Lionel. This she did for the sole purpose of being able to find out from him in a seemly manner whether the song had been composed for her or for someone else.

CHAPTER IX

How on that New Year's Day Lionel Was Left Out Once More by the Maiden Angeline Who Then Mockingly Gave Him a Golden Thread from Her Weaving Frame.

On New Year's Day Lady Angeline ordered Lionel, her page, to call all of the household to her apartments at an appointed hour so that they might receive their New Year gift from her. Lionel was very eager to do so, for he had high hopes that Lady Angeline would bestow upon him not the least of the presents since he was in her personal service and was always at her beck and call.

The whole household gathered in haste, and after they were all assembled, Angeline proceeded to give out the New Year gifts, from the first to the last. When it came to Lionel's turn, however, she said: "I most certainly have forgotten you, Lionel! But be patient this time; I will reward you doubly another year." But this she actually did only to find out how the lad would react. Lionel turned away from the maiden with a deep sigh, for her words had pierced him no less than if a keen sword had been plunged into his heart. He was so ashamed that he felt compelled to leave her chamber, and then he fell to crying heartily, lamenting his grief and wretchedness.

The next day, upon resuming his duty in Angeline's chamber, he stood before the maiden who was expertly weaving an exquisite pattern. Lionel kept sighing from the bottom of his heart as often as he gazed at her. She was well aware of this but did not show it, for most of her maidens were still in the apartment with her. Therefore, she bided her time until they left.

Lionel, however, could not forget his misery and was completely given to deep sighs, which he often let escape from his heart. When at last Angeline was all alone in her chamber with Lionel, she addressed him with smiling lips and friendly words. "My dear Lionel," she said, "you must know that I would like to ask you two questions. The first one pertains to an occurrence which took place last summer, namely that song about wretchedness; my question is whether you or someone else composed it and whom it concerns. The other is the following: what moved you to such deep sighs today and yesterday? You must not withhold from me anything about these matters."

The youth did not remain silent for long. "Noble and gracious lady," he answered at once, "I am ready to answer both your questions. First of all, I composed that song myself, and your grace is the only reason for it, for a year ago your grace bestowed presents upon all of the household, as you did again yesterday, but left out only me, the poor kitchen apprentice. And now that I have entered your service, I would never have thought that your grace would overlook me again as you did last year. These are the only causes for my sorrow."

When Angeline heard these explanations from Lionel, she bethought herself of how she might give the good youth further reason to complain so that perhaps he might compose yet another song about her. She also decided to requite him very richly shortly afterwards. She reached for a twined gold thread that was hanging from her weaving frame and gave it to Lionel. "You shall not be able to say any longer that I ignored you when I rewarded the rest of the household, my dear page," she said mockingly, "therefore, accept from me this rich gift as a present and reward and keep it well so that next year you may show me how well you took care of it.

Lionel accepted the golden thread with great joy and thanked the maiden most warmly. "Gracious lady," he said, "I will preserve this gift of yours in such a manner, and care for it so well, that I shall never lose it."

"Do so," said Angeline, "and thus you give me a good reason to bestow another present upon you."

This is what Lady Angeline told the young man; but she had no knowledge at all of the boundless love he had for her. Moreover, she had no idea whatsoever as to where he would preserve the golden thread. Lionel, however, took leave of her and hastened to his room.

CHAPTER X
❦ How Lionel Repaired to His Room, Opened His Breast with a Pen-knife, Sewed Up in It the Golden Thread and Sealed His Wound with Costly Poultices and Ointments.

When Lionel was sure that he was alone, he took a sharp pen-knife, bared his chest, incised the skin of the left side, took the golden thread and lay it between skin and flesh; then, suffering no little pain, he stitched his skin back together with a needle he had prepared beforehand. The love for the maiden, however, had such a powerful grip upon him that he paid little attention to pain. He had also asked the surgeon for ointments and good healing poultices before he had wounded himself. And thus his wound healed so well in a short time that he felt but little pain.

When he did resume his duty in her chamber, Angeline studied him very carefully to see whether he showed any sign of melancholy as before, but all she could see was a happy disposition.

Since he often had to sing for the maiden's pleasure, he thought to himself: "Now I have the opportunity to open my heart to lady Angeline in secret and without anyone else knowing of it." And so he undertook to compose a song about the golden thread and to sing it in the maidens' apartment. He surmised that since Lady Angeline had seen through his other ditty so well, she would also ponder this one. With such thoughts he composed the following song:

(To the tune of "Ach Lieb mit Leid"*)

> One year ago
> Pain and sorrow
> Dwelled within this heart of mine.
> But this very year
> A tiny thread
> Made of golden thread
> Destroyed my woe
> And made me grow
> Out of all sorrow and pain.
> How glad am I
> That now I may
> Sing, frolic, and laugh again!

> This very thread
> I did inset
> Into my heart right away,
> And no one may
> By night or day
> Attempt to take it away.
> In a strong shrine—
> This heart of mine—
> There do I preserve this thread.
> He who wants it
> Must, to take it,
> First of all cleave my breast.

---

*According to Bondzio, the indication of the melody must be a mistake, for the song "Ach Lieb mit Leid," "Oh Love with Sorrow," has a completely different verse scheme.

> The fairest of all
> Gave me this thread
> And with it great joy indeed!
> Not for gold, stone,
> Or any money
> Would I ever part
> With that thread of mine!
> It is so fine
> That though it should bring me harm
> I shall in spite of the pain
> Always remain
> Loyal to this this yarn.

Lionel learned this song very quickly, and whenever Angeline exhorted him to sing, he would sing first of the golden thread, and other songs only afterwards. Angeline, who was a clever maiden, kept wondering where Lionel could have preserved it, for she knew quite well that the youth had composed the song about the exalted thread all by himself. Therefore, she decided to find out everything from the youth himself as soon as she had an opportunity to be alone with him.

One Sunday Angeline pretended to be sick. She sent her maidens to church but ordered that Lionel be left on duty before the door. Now when she surmised that she was quite safe, she summoned Lionel, who came at once. "My dear Lionel," she said, "tell me, do you still have in your possession the golden thread I gave you from my frame? If you do, I entreat you to show it to me; in exchange I shall bestow upon you a more costly present."

"Gracious lady," said the youth, "the key to unlock the vessel in which the thread is hidden is in my room. Should your grace so wish, I shall fetch it at once."

"This is my wish and desire," said the maiden, "but it must be right now."

Lionel hastened to his room, grasped a sharp pen-knife and nimbly returned to Angeline's chamber. There he opened the front of his doublet, and before she realized what he was about, he deftly incised his healed wound and quite undaunted pulled the golden thread from it.

At that sight, Angeline was greatly frightened, for Lionel was bleeding quite profusely. She took the knife and the golden thread away from him and said: "You must hurry to the doctor and have your wound dressed at once lest greater harm befall you!"

"Gracious lady," said Lionel, "you must not worry about my wound. I dressed it myself the first time and, with your leave, I shall go do so again."

"Do that," said Angeline, "and then return."

With great joy Lionel took leave of the maiden whom he loved so ardently that he felt no pain whatsoever from his wound. He quickly dressed his wound, changed his clothes and disposed of the bloody garments.

After Lionel had left her, Angeline took the golden thread and washed it in clear water. There it was! As shiny as if it had just been taken off the frame. The maiden could not marvel enough at this. But she marveled even more at the youth who twice had injured his very flesh with a sharp knife for her sake. From then on Angeline was indeed grievously wounded by Cupid's arrow. She waited with great longing for the youth, to see whether he had become pale or weak. When he returned shortly afterwards with a cheerful countenance, she rejoiced no little at the sight of him.

By now it was about time for the maidens to return from church, and Angeline could no longer converse with Lionel about what filled her heart. "Dear Lionel," she said, therefore, "do not ask now for the present I promised you. There is not enough time for that, but tomorrow, in full view of all my maidens, I shall give you a little package with instructions for delivery. You must not heed that order but take the package straight to your room and keep it for yourself in all good faith. There will also be a letter with it; take it to heart and heed what it says. But now, go stand before my chamber and wait at the door, for my maidens will certainly not be much longer."

Lionel made haste to do as he was told. He had been standing before the door but a short while when the maidens returned from church.

CHAPTER XI
🍎 *How the Next Day Angeline Wrote Lionel a Letter in Her Most Private Chamber, and How She Gave It to Him, along with Many Costly Jewels.*

Angeline could think of nothing else but Lionel. She often thought of the great pain he must have suffered for her sake, and of which she no longer needed proof, for she had seen with her own eyes how he had incised his breast and pulled the golden thread from it. Thus she spent the remainder of that day in a daze, of which her maidens grew aware and worried lest she be very sick but wished to remain silent about it. Therefore, they secretly gathered in council. One of them, named Cordelia, the daughter of a knight, addressed them thus: "My dearest companions, can there be one among us who has so little understanding that she fails to notice how much our gracious lady changed? This is certainly caused by a grave and dangerous disease. I can also see that she does not want to distress us, and even though she always behaves cheerfully toward us, she certainly does so with a heavy and afflicted heart. Therefore, I propose quite sincerely that we entreat our gracious lady to let us know what causes her to be so sick and uncomfortable, for should matters end less than well, our lord, her father, may make us answer for it dearly."

The maidens praised this proposition and decided to go see Angeline at once. Cordelia, who was particularly fond of her lady, spoke for them all in a kind and devoted manner. "Most gracious lady," she said, "because of the great love and devotion we bear you, we feel that we should find out from you the cause of your melancholy, for truly, we worry greatly that you should think us unworthy of your trust. Therefore, dearest lady, we beg and entreat you most humbly to tell us the cause of your melancholy thoughts, for, who knows, we may be able to devise some counsel to relieve you."

"My trusted maidens," answered Lady Angeline, "you must not be vexed because of my foolishness, for I hope to God that this humor will be over before long. Therefore, I beg you kindly not to disturb me today so that I may enjoy some rest in my private chamber." Thus, she dimissed her maidens, and they withdrew from her apartment.

Lionel, her devoted doorman, stood before the outer door of her apartment, waiting patiently and hoping every time he heard her door open that his beloved Angeline would call him in. But she was sitting in her chamber, writing the following letter: "With all my heart I wish you the best of luck and fortune, my most beloved Lionel. I can no longer conceal from you the deep and burning love I bear you in all modesty and honor, for when you cut open your chest and pulled out of it the golden thread, you so completely caught and bound my fancy that I will be yours, even if thus I should have to renounce all of my father's possessions. For I know full well that all my father's possessions could never buy a love like yours.

"Should you be willing to heed my instructions, I shall impart to you expedient ways in which the two of us might live together for a long time with the good will and blessing of my father. I know you to be of such marvelous understanding and skills that I am sure you will ingratiate yourself with my father and find in him a gracious lord. Nevertheless, my most beloved one, you must keep this matter totally secret and let no one become so intimate or dear to you as to confide to him our love. Be assured of the same from me, and as a token of our steadfastness and constancy, accept from me this ring which I cherish dearly, for it was the very last thing my mother gave to me on her deathbed.

Treasure it for her sake, but also because you love me, of which I have no doubt whatsoever.

"The other gifts and presents which you will find in this package are your New Year gift in exchange of the golden thread. I beg you not to hold them in contempt because of their worthlessness, for you shall receive many more from me. My beloved Lionel, if ever you should have a request of me, you may address it to me in writing at any time. Herewith, I commend you to God. May He keep you in good health!"

When Angeline had folded this letter and sealed it with her signet ring, she took it and wrapped it up in a small package together with the ring, a fine shirt, and a smart béret. Since now the evening was at hand, her maidens returned to inquire about her well-being. They found her quite cheerful and of good complexion, which pleased them greatly. When the evening came to a close and the stars were strewn across the dark blue skies, everyone went to bed and slumbered away the night most sweetly.

CHAPTER XII
❧ *How Angeline Gave Lionel the Little Package in the Presence of All Her Maidens.*

Aurora, the noble rosiness of dawn, cheerfully ushered in the new day. The nightingale and the other little birds announced it just as cheerfully. Angeline got up, dressed daintily and sat at a window to listen to the song of the birds, which put her in quite a sprightly disposition. Lionel, however, had spent a sleepless night, for he could hardly await the morning to find out what present the maiden would bestow upon him. He got up, dressed in his best clothes, and betook himself to the garden very cheerfully. Not knowing that Angeline, his most beloved maiden, was already up and sitting at a window, he went to his usual place in the rose bower. There he began to sing most happily. Angeline perceived this immediately and listened with great joy to the song of her beloved.

Perchance gazing through the hedge, Lionel espied his beloved maiden at the window, playing with a very beautiful little lapdog and a parrot, listening attentively to his song. Lionel was absolutely elated when he knew his maiden to be present. He spared no effort as he sang, continuing until it seemed time to go fulfill his duties. Then he left the garden and went to Lady Angeline's apartment.

Meanwhile, Angeline's maidens arrived, as was their custom. As soon as they had entered her apartment and bidden Angeline good morning, she thanked them cordially and asked them at once whether young Lionel was standing before her chamber. They said that he was there. "Then call him in at once," said Angeline, "he is to bring my lord and father something he needs."

They called in the youth, who entered with great joy, as if stepping out of a dark vault and suddenly beholding the bright sunshine. Thus he felt as he beheld the maiden. Duly bowing, he bade a day full of happiness and bliss first to her and then to all her companions as well. Angeline, who was no less delighted by his presence, began to tease him. "My dear Lionel," she said in jest, "why not tell me what drove you out of your bed so early this morning and caused you to sing so happily and so well, for the nightingale, the thrush, and the other birds of the forest did not precede you by much. You joined them very soon with your own sweet voice, and I could not help but listen to you, heart and soul. And even though you obviously did not sing in my service, I don't mind. But the maiden whom you serve in such a manner must reward you, which she certainly will; otherwise, I should say she has very little understanding and a heart of stone. Tell me, dear Lionel, which one of these maidens here aroused and awakened you so very early? I will make her my favorite!"

The maidens could not but marvel at the jesting words of Angeline, and they kept looking at one another, blushing with shame, for each one thought that Angeline had been talking about her. Lionel was no less ashamed, but blushing made him look twice as handsome.

Now when Angeline had teased him long enough, he gave her the following answer: "Most gracious lady, I take your jesting lightly, but since your grace asks me for which one of the maidens I was singing, I must tell you that on this earth there is and will be only one to whom I have opened my heart, and she knows that I am and will be at her service and hers only. I will serve her assiduously and steadfastly till the day I die. But I fully acknowledge that it is not becoming that I strive for the love of such noble maidens as are at your court, for the poor youth that I am is not good enough for them. But still, my poverty and my low birth will never keep me from serving maidens and ladies, for I have faith in an old proverb that says: 'Never did one serve ladies in vain; the one requites what the other spurns.' "

Never before had the maidens noticed how handsome Lionel really was, for on that very day, he had dressed particularly well. Besides, his complexion was white by nature; his body was tall, straight, and well-formed; his brow bold and intrepid; his hair beautiful and curling delicately like spun gold. His chest was strong, and on the whole, he was not only the most handsome youth at court, but he also surpassed them all in stature, beauty, and virtue.

Angeline took the little package she had made up for him and handed it to him in the presence of all her maidens, saying, "Dear Lionel, take this package and bring it to my lord and father. Tell him it contains what he asked me to send to him. After you have delivered it, return to our company so that we may chat some more; and don't let it vex you if we tease you, for who knows how I or my maidens may requite you in all modesty and honor!"

"Gracious lady," answered Lionel, "your teasing is a special honor and pleasure for me."

Thus, he left the maiden, full of joy. He could hardly wait to reach his quarters, so that he might find out what was hidden in his little package. Upon opening it, he cast not a single glance at the presents until he had read the maiden's letter to his heart's content, kissing it oft and passionately. Only then did he examine the jewels and the ring in which was set a beautiful blue sapphire. With this color, the maiden wished to convey to him the constancy of her love. He took the ring, hung it at once around his neck and said: "Now rejoice, Lionel, for this very hour fortune has raised you very high. Who on earth could be happier than I, the blissful Lionel? Oh you, dearest father, dear mother, and dearest of all, you my providers, my godfather and his wife, I wish to God that my good fortune could be known to you so that you could rejoice and delight with me! Ah! If now my classmates who elected me as their king knew of my good fortune, they certainly would greatly rejoice. This, however, cannot and should not happen yet, since my beloved maiden has forbidden it solemnly. But should God and fortune lend me their grace, one day I shall share my joy with all of mine!"

When Lionel had rejoiced enough over these rich presents and gifts, he undressed, donned the beautiful shirt Angeline had bestowed upon him and returned to the maidens with whom he engaged in much merrymaking and jesting. Thereafter, it did not take long for him to be held in high esteem by all the maidens, who were never really happy unless Lionel was present.

These conditions lasted until Lionel grew tall and strong of body. Then the count removed him from the maiden's apartment and took him as his valet. Lionel and Angeline were deeply afflicted thereby. No longer could they be close and intimate with the same good reasons and pretexts as before, even though he saw the maiden more often than any other servant at the court, since the count sent Lionel to his daughter at all times for whatever he needed from her or sent to her. But still, their great love was quite unknown to him.

CHAPTER XIII
How Lionel Became the Count's Valet and Was Sent on an Errand. How He Became Lost in a Wood. How He Found a Beautiful Hunting Dog, and What Strange Adventures Befell Him Because of This Dog.

After Lionel had been taken from the service of his maiden and had become the count's valet, he behaved so well that his lord entrusted him with all his business and also conferred with him at all times for every matter he undertook. One day, it came to pass that the count had sent Lionel on a long and distant journey to another count among his relatives. On his way, Lionel came to a huge forest in which he became utterly lost and wandered a whole day with very little knowledge as to where he might be. Toward evening, he heard a cart at a distance, from which he inferred that game was being hunted in the forest. He gathered comfort therefrom, hoping to come across hunters who might show him the way out of the forest.

Shortly afterwards, a beautiful white hunting dog came bounding toward him. Its leash had snapped, but its collar was still there. It had been in hot pursuit of a stag, but had lost its scent when it had escaped through a large body of water. As soon as the hunting dog noticed Lionel, it ran up to him and leapt at him full of excitement. Lionel gently stroked the dog. "My dear friend," he said, "if only you could understand my words, I would ask you to lead me out of these wretched woods."

The hunting dog, however, wanted to stay with Lionel and showed no intention of returning to the hunting wagon. When Lionel noticed this, he decided to ride in the direction from which the hunting dog had come, hoping to find the hunters. The dog followed cheerfully, then started running ahead of the horse until it led them onto a well-kept path that ran between the game reservation and a mighty body of water.

Then they came to a clearing where the hunters had built a great fire. Lionel dismounted and found hay and fodder, which the hunters' horses had left uneaten. He gave it to his horse, which made do with it. Then, Lionel spent the whole night there because he worried that otherwise he might stray even deeper into the forest.

When the night was over and the next day dawned in the sky, Lionel mounted up and rode until he reached the edge of the forest. Then he followed a road that led him to a bridge spanning a large stream; he noticed a small house on the other side. An old man was sitting in front of it, mending his nets and his fishing lines. Lionel rode up to him and greeted him very kindly, for which the old man thanked him. "Dear father," said Lionel, "I entreat you to give me directions so that I may return among people. I have been wandering in that forest since yesterday morning, and I have no idea in what kind of lands I may be or who is lord over them."

The good man took great pity upon him and asked if he had eaten anything during that time. "Nothing at all," said Lionel, "and that is why I wish all the more to return among people, so that I may still my hunger!"

"Dismount then," said the old man, "my wife will prepare you something to eat." Lionel accepted very gratefully, dismounted, and entered the small house of the fisherman, whose wife cooked for him such good things as she had. Lionel ate with a hearty appetite. When he was well satisfied, he rewarded the fisherman's wife, remounted his horse, thanked the old man very kindly for the food and asked him for the right road, which was pointed out to him very respectfully. Then Lionel rode forth to accomplish his mission. When he had carried it out, he rode back home through the country in which he had found the beautiful hunting dog.

The lord of the forest had been very sorry about the loss of his hunting dog and had sent to inquire in the neighboring cities, towns, and boroughs in the hope of finding out anything about it. Perchance, Lionel had to spend a night with an innkeeper who also had received instructions about the animal. Expecting no trouble, Lionel stabled his horse then repaired to the main room with the hunting dog. The innkeeper received him with friendly words but with a false heart because he had recognized the dog all too well. He ordered one of his servants quickly to mount a nag and ride to the lord of the forest to report that the animal had been found and that he should immediately send a messenger to claim it, for the one who had it was an insolent fellow, and he dared not take it away from him by himself.

CHAPTER XIV

 How Lionel Was Assaulted by a Servant of the Lord of the Forest during the Evening Meal; How He Found Himself in Great Peril but Still Managed to Escape with the Hunting Dog.

According to an old proverb, "An honest host is a godsend to his guest, but a scoundrel's house is a godforsaken place." This was also true for the good lad: he did not expect any mischief and thought that he had found a good host, but he was betrayed by him.

As soon as the lord of the forest heard from the innkeeper's servant about the whereabouts of the pointer, he at once dispatched one of his servants, a carefully chosen, stout-hearted horseguard.

Lionel was sitting at a table, the pointer beside him on the bench, when the servant entered and called the hunting dog by its name, "True." But the animal refused to stir from Lionel's side. This deeply vexed the horseguard. He drew close to Lionel and said, full of arrogance, "You good-for-nothing you! How can you so maliciously steal my master's favorite dog? Let me tell you that you will derive no benefit from it. Think it over and give back the dog if you care for your hide."

"Good fellow," said Lionel, "you accuse me of a foul deed, and I'm not going to stand for it, because I never presumed to steal this hunting dog. I was utterly lost in the forest when this noble animal came to me and led me out of that wretched forest. And after that, it stayed with me without either leash or line, and now it follows me about freely."

"A curse on you!" said the horseguard, "It is clear that you cast a spell on this dog, but you will regret it." And with these words he whipped out a pair of brass knuckles, thinking to knock Lionel to the floor. But the latter was not idle; he jumped from the table, whipped out his good sword, and pressed the horseguard so hard that the latter had to give ground under his blows.

When the treacherous innkeeper saw this, he rushed to the help of the horseguard in order to protect him. Lionel noticed him at once and turned against him with such rage that the first blow he landed on the traitor's head felled him to the floor with a loud cry. Then, Lionel turned back to the horseguard, but the latter was already on his horse, raising such a clamor in the village that the peasants were massing. When Lionel saw this, he told himself, "No sense waiting around!" He hastened to his horse, mounted, and rode hard, for he worried lest great harm befall him should the peasants catch him.

Now when the groom returned without the hunting dog, his lord was very wroth. But the groom dared not tell him how he had fared with the animal and Lionel, for he worried that he would become a laughingstock; therefore, he was as brief as possible. There are many such braggarts who claim they can destroy the whole world with a single hit, but when someone stands up to them, it is usually the road they hit. This is exactly what this horseguard did; he used his horse's hooves as his armor and defense.

Lionel, the good youth, had ridden off without either taking leave of his host or asking anyone for the shortest way home. Nevertheless, he used a compass that he carried with him and that gave him bearings from which he easily gathered whether he was riding north, south, east, or west. Thus, he kept riding until he came to a friary in which there lived an old friar, a pious, good, and trustworthy man.

In a loud voice Lionel called out: "Should anyone live here, please be so kind as to help me with directions, for I am lost." The hermit came out at once. He welcomed Lionel very kindly and asked him whereto he was traveling, which the youth told him in detail. "Dear friend," said the friar, "you have strayed far from your road, and, in all truth, you will never be able to reach an inn within three hours. Therefore, I urge you to dismount while I bring you some bread, good meat, and fresh, clear water so that you may refresh yourself a little." Lionel accepted this offer gratefully and dismounted. The friar laid him a little table under a green tree in front of his house and served bread and meat so good and tasty that it seemed to Lionel he had not feasted so well in a long time, for it was now well past noon, and hunger had been his companion for quite a while. The friar gave the horse a small measure of barley and also took care of the hunting dog.

When Lionel had well satisfied his hunger, he asked the hermit for the reckoning, but the latter would not hear of it. Lionel, however, forced him to accept some money against his will. Then, he remounted and rode off in the direction the good friar had pointed out to him.

We shall now let him ride on, and we shall go back to his father and mother and his godfather who had brought him up, and how they had fared after Lionel's departure.

CHAPTER XV

How Herman Sent for Erik and His Wife, Who Were Keeping Cattle in the Pastures; How He Asked Them to Render Account, for They Had Not Done So in Many Years; How Erik Was Comforted by His Wife Felicia.

You have heard how Lionel fled without taking leave either from his father and mother, nor from his godfather and his wife. By now they were in the eighth year without having heard from him and knew not whether he was dead or alive. His father and mother daily lamented his departure because all these years they had worried that the merchant Herman might think that they had known about their son's flight and deprive them of their farm. But they worried quite in vain, for Herman had well understood from the letter that Lionel had left behind that the herdsman and his wife had had no knowledge of the boy's departure.

One day Herman sent news to his tenant Erik that he was to confer with his wife, for he was to render account within a few days. As soon as Erik and his wife Felicia heard this, they feared exceedingly, for they had not rendered an account in many years, nor had their landlord ever required one. "Oh God!" said Erik, "now that which caused me to worry for so many long years has happened. Why am I no longer in my old office? We could now be sitting quietly in our own humble house. After keeping my cattle during the day, I would be at the end of all my worries. Happy is he who lives in poverty but is free and is not accountable to anyone.

"Anyone who holds an office, a charge, or a function, and who tries to be fair to all, will be cheated by base and false people. By flattering and cunning words, they induce him to trust them, to lend them money and to extend them credit; but the rent grows into a very large sum, and then comes the landlord from whom he holds his charge; he wants to settle accounts with his steward and be paid, which is but fair. But oh! God! The rent from that steward's tenants is still outstanding; the landlord becomes angry with him and turns him out. Besides, now and then there are borrowers who are so unscrupulous that they swear great oaths and pledge their honor that they have repaid their debt, which, in fact, they never intended to do.

"But should a steward be tough, severe, and businesslike, and should he claim in due time what belongs by right to his master, everyone chides him and calls him a dog, a tyrant, and a madcap. This is true for any tenant managing a landlord's farm. As long as the landlord receives everything according to his fancy, and as long as his farm, pastures, fields, and cattle yield great surpluses, the tenant is held in esteem; but should his crops fail, or should a disease befall his cattle so that there is a loss, the tenant is immediately held unworthy, and the landlord lays all the blame on him. Then he is accused of having tilled the fields poorly, of not having dunged them, or of having left the cattle unattended.

"As for me, I testify in truth that I have served my master in all honesty, that I have taken care of his business with the utmost loyalty, and that I have maintained his property most carefully. But still it is not possible for me, a simple peasant not acquainted with writing, to render an account, since my landlord has not asked one of me for many years. Oh, my dear Felicia, give me your good and loyal advice as to how we are to behave in this matter, for I don't feel wise enough myself. Were it only God's will that Lionel be present! We would never have come in such dire straits. But I am afraid that our landlord thinks that we knew something about our son's flight."

A loyal advisor to her husband, Felicia said: "My dear Erik, do not fret about the message of our dear landlord and patron, for I know quite well that he will not expect anything impossible from us, and even less ask for it. When I paid him a visit on the last market day, I sensed nothing but kindness in him. He inquired very warmly about you and how you were, if you were well and healthy, and especially if we had had any news from our son Lionel. I answered him in all modesty, and also entreated him not to avenge upon us Lionel's disobedience, since we knew nothing about it. Upon this, both our lord and his wife said: 'We are well aware of this, for Lionel left us a letter in which he clearly explained his intentions.' 'However,' our lord also said, 'I have good and high hopes that I shall not die before I see Lionel again, and,' he added, 'I have high hopes that Lionel is well and prosperous, for I have had many a pleasant dream about him lately.'"

With these and similar words, Felicia comforted her husband so well that in the end he was convinced that his case would stand successfully before his landlord. When the appointed day arrived, Erik and his wife went to their dear patrons in the city. They were received quite honorably and well, which greatly comforted Erik and put an end to his sadness.

CHAPTER XVI
How the Tenant Erik Received Many Gifts from His Landlord Who Renewed His Lease and Made It Hereditary.

Herman, the merchant, had a good meal prepared. He invited to it many honorable guests as well as Erik and his wife. Now when they were all assembled, they washed their hands, sat down at the table, and gave thanks to the Lord for the food which he daily provided for them. Thereupon, the servants graciously brought in delicate and well-prepared dishes, while others served drinks in vessels from beautiful sideboards.

About halfway through the meal, Herman addressed the gathering and said, turning to his tenant: "My most favorite and faithful servant Erik, I know full well what faithful and diligent services you have performed for me these last twenty years. I receive proof daily that the farm that I entrusted to you with all its dependencies is very prosperous and has greatly increased in value. Furthermore, its livestock never decreased but has multiplied so well that I was able to sell many a head.

"I truly believe that the Lord often increases and multiplies the possessions of those who have great properties because of his love for their servants. Thus, Laban was blessed in everything he undertook because Jacob was his son-in-law, and likewise, much good befell Potiphar because of Joseph. All this leads me to think that God lets me prosper—and that he has increased my possessions—because of your faithful service. Therefore, dear Erik, let me know how many head of cattle, small or large, there are presently on your farm. Then deliver half to me and keep the other half for yourself. I want to share with you in the same manner all the green crops in your fields, pastures, and meadows. Furthermore, I give you and your children all my properties, together with the farm, as a hereditary tenancy at a low rent. This promise I give to you in the presence of all these gentle folks and good friends." Thereupon, Herman offered his tenant Erik and his wife Felicia his right hand as a token of his pledge.

Who could have been happier than Erik and his wife? They had come expecting hard reckonings, but now they had been granted their own cattle! Their joy was so heartfelt that both of them began crying profusely and not knowing how to thank their landlord and his wife. But after they had returned to their farm, they devoted themselves to very faithful management and kept thanking God for his great kindness. Everything they undertook turned to their advantage. This lasted until their son Lionel returned, and then their standing improved even more. And now, let us return to Lionel.

CHAPTER XVII
🍎 *How Lionel Returned Home, Bringing with Him the Beautiful Hunting Dog; How Angeline Had Him Tell Her Everything that Happened to Him, Especially How He Had Come by the Hunting Dog.*

Now free of all his worries, Lionel returned home very cheerfully, bringing with him his beautiful hunting dog. When he had reported to his master everything he had accomplished, he went to his quarters and changed clothes before paying a visit to his maiden. She was already aware of his arrival and wasted no time before sending one of her most trusted maidens to him. He hastened to her apartment, where she received him very kindly, inquiring about the cause of his long absence, which he gave in great detail. "Lionel," she said then, "where did you acquire that beautiful dog? Where did you find it?"

Since the maiden showed so much interest in the hunting dog, Lionel thought: "It is certainly not without reason that she wishes to know it. Perhaps she thinks that I have stolen it, or that I have wrongfully taken it from someone." He said, therefore, "Gracious lady, I cannot keep from you anything you want to know. Understand then that when I was riding on business for my gracious lord, I was led by accident or chance into a huge and mighty forest in which I became lost so completely that I could not find my way out of it. But when I had resigned myself to spending the night in the forest, this noble animal appeared, showing great friendliness toward me.

"I adopted the dog, hoping that it might lead me out of the forest. It returned the same way it had come; I rode after it, and very soon it led me to a well-laid and well-kept path running between a fine game reservation and a great river over which there was no bridge of any kind, nor could I distinguish a ford crossing it. But as night was falling, we came to a clearing in which hunters had fed their horses, and in which a big fire was still burning. I decided to spend the night there. In a feeding trough, I found some fodder that the hunters' horses had left. I tied my tired horse over it, and it had plenty to eat. We spent the night the best we could, but as soon as day broke, I remounted my horse. The hunting dog kept running in front of me, and finally we came out of the forest on a wide road that led us to a bridge, on the other side of which there dwelled a poor fisherman. I told him of my hunger, and in no time at all his wife had prepared some food."

But for the sake of brevity, let it be said that Lionel told the maiden in great detail everything that had happened to him with the treacherous innkeeper, the horseguard, and the friar.

Angeline kept marveling at the adventure with the dog and said: "Really, Lionel, you must never forget the loyalty and the friendship of this noble animal. I shall make it a nice collar which I want it to wear on account of its loyalty. Because of this very loyalty, you shall call it from now on by no other name than 'True.'" Lionel promised her to do so.

CHAPTER XVIII
🍂 *How Angeline Very Artfully Embroidered a Nice Collar with Clusters of Pearls, and How Lionel Presented the Hunting Dog to the Maiden, Who Cared for It Most Tenderly.*

Angeline and Lionel delighted each other with talk, and when it seemed time to part company, the youth took leave of her and went to perform his duty in his master's apartment. After he had left, the maiden did not waste much time; she went to her room immediately, took fine pearls, velvet, and silk, and began to embroider a rich and fine collar with a beautiful cluster of pearls on each side. She adorned it with gilt clasps and fastened it with a gilt buckle.

After the collar was finished, she called into her private chamber one of her favorite and most trusted maidens. "Most trusted and dearest Florence," she told her, "I entreat you not to be different from what you have always been when I have opened my heart to you, and to repair to young Lionel as soon as you can. Tell him to accompany you to my apartment together with his beautiful hunting dog as soon as his business will allow, for I have made his dog this collar with my own hands, and I want to put it on myself." Florence did not waste any time carrying out lady Angeline's orders.

Perchance looking through a window opening on the garden, she caught sight of Lionel playing with his hunting dog. She greatly rejoiced at this sight, for she would not waste any time looking for him. At once she ran down the stairs joyfully and came into the garden. Lionel noticed the maiden at once, and he knew immediately from her countenance that she was looking for him. He cheerfully approached her and bowed. Florence apprised him at once of Angeline's wish, a message the youth received with great joy. He delayed but little and accompanied Florence to Angeline's apartment.

Angeline received him with kind words. She took the collar and put it around the hunting dog's neck, saying, "My most beloved Lionel, I promised that I would make this collar for your dog, and although it is not wrought very artistically, I still have high hopes that you would suffer this noble animal to wear it and that you would take great care of it. Although you don't know what it was first named, you should call it nothing else than 'True.' Thus, you will please me greatly."

Lionel answered civilly and with a happy heart: "Most beloved lady, I very humbly thank your grace for this present, and your wish shall be my command."

"That is my wish," said Angeline, "and I really would be sorry if you should lose this noble animal."

Lionel could well infer from those words that she actually fancied the dog for herself. He took it by its collar and led it to her, saying, "Dear and gracious lady, if it is not too much trouble for your grace, I would beg you most humbly to accept this hunting dog as a present from me. It would not be possible for me to keep it, since my master sends me away more often and farther than any other of his servants. Should I then lose this dog together with its collar, and should your grace be afflicted by its loss, I should greatly regret ever having laid my eyes upon it. Therefore, I beg your grace to accept this fine animal from me."

"This I do gladly," said Angeline, "and I shall also take very good care of that fine and noble animal. But I shall requite you for this rich present, my dear Lionel."

Many kind words were thus exchanged between Lionel, Angeline, and the other maidens until the time of the evening meal. When the bell was rung in the yard, calling the whole household to the evening meal, Lionel took leave of his beloved maiden and then endeavored to fulfill his duty as usual. But now, we shall return to Herman, the merchant, and see how his beloved son fared.

CHAPTER XIX

How the Merchant's Legitimate Son Earnestly Entreated His Father to Allow Him to Go Search for His Dearest Brother Lionel. How the Father Was Very Reluctant to Allow It but Finally Agreed.

Above, you learned how the merchant brought up Lionel very well and honestly together with his own son and heir called Walter. The latter mourned for a long time after the departure of his adopted companion and brother. After Lionel had left, he resolved that, should God allow him to reach maturity, he would not fail to search for his dearest brother and companion, no matter in what country he might be. Lionel, however, longed no less for him and had resolved to visit his companion and brother unbeknownst to all and, if possible, to entice him away from his country.

By now, Walter, the merchant's son, had grown into a very tall, handsome, and well-educated young man. One day he approached his father with chosen words. "My father," he said, "I beg you kindly to grant me a small request, for I can rest neither day nor night if I don't learn or find out what happened to my dearest brother and first companion; I mean Lionel, whom you reared with and beside me and in the same love. Therefore, I entreat you to provide me with a small allowance and a horse so that I may search for my dearest brother and friend. At the same time I shall see the world and learn its ways. You must not worry about my getting into mischief, dear father, or about my wasting uselessly what I have, or even about my falling in with wicked and worthless company. Thanks to God, my teacher at school has taught me well enough the effects of bad company so that I shall shun and avoid it for the rest of my days. All I request of you, dear father, is that you allow me to undertake this journey."

The merchant was not a little downcast at the words of his son. He did not want to deny his request, but he did not want to grant it, either. Therefore, he addressed his son very kindly, saying: "Oh! Walter, my only and most beloved son, you must not inflict such wretchedness upon your father and your dear mother. As for me, I am afraid that Lionel, for whom you intend to search, has perished long ago, for I have no doubt that, were he alive, he would have sent us a message long ago, since he was quite aware of the great love and friendship we bore him. Therefore, if he is no longer alive, all your trouble and efforts would be in vain. But if he is still alive and has relegated us to utter oblivion, why should you bother to search for him in foreign lands? Stay with us, your father and your mother, and look to other company for pleasure and fun, because I am afraid that Lionel is no longer alive."

When Walter heard his beloved father's words, he did not wish to obey, no matter how obedient he had been up to this point. He kept pressing his father not to deny his request, assuring him that he would not tarry on his way and would return as soon as possible. When the father saw that his son could not be deterred, he finally gave in and granted his request. The youth made himself ready at once.

When the matter became known to his mother, she was quite aggrieved, but Herman comforted her as well as he could. He gave his son a good allowance and also hired him a trustworthy and reliable servant to ride with him and take care of him. Thus, the good youth Walter, together with his scrvant, left his father and mother, having on his mind nothing else but to find Lionel.

CHAPTER XX
❦ How Walter and His Servant Were Robbed in the Woods by Three Wicked Fellows; How They Were Stripped and Tied to a Tree.

By now, Walter and his servant had been riding close to a fortnight. Everywhere they asked for Lionel, but no one could give them a proper answer, for young Lionel had not identified himself anywhere. Therefore, nobody knew anything about him. Moreover, he had already become a tall and comely horseman, a match for any enemy. Walter, however, thought he had carried on with school and studies, and, therefore, asked for Lionel in all the schools whenever he came to a city.

One day, the two youths had to ride through a huge, thick forest, the prospect of which really terrified them. On the outskirts of the woods, there was an inn, a public house in which merchants would gather until enough of them were assembled so that they might ride safely through the forest, for many murders and robberies took place in it.

The innkeeper very honestly warned the two youths not to venture on the way alone but to wait for more merchants to come. This warning was overheard by three wicked thugs who were staying at the inn. They pretended to be gem traders intent on traveling to Lisbon to buy precious stones; they also feigned great fear. The innkeeper was filled with pity, for he believed them, and thus he said: "Friends, be patient; I hope that tomorrow there will arrive several merchants with whom you may travel safely."

But when the three thugs heard about the merchants who were to come, they worried lest the two youths should elude them. Therefore, they agreed among themselves that the oldest one of them, a very cunning scoundrel, would pretend to be tired of waiting any longer, and to be willing to take his chances: since never before he had come to harm in this forest, he claimed, he had high hopes of being lucky again on this trip. His two companions chimed in, saying: "In that case we shall take a chance with you."

When Walter and his companion heard this, they believed the concoctions of the wily fellows and asked to be accepted in their company. But the scoundrels pretended to be reluctant and said: "We would not be able to keep up with you since you are on horseback and the three of us are on foot." "Well my friends," replied Walter, "If you accept us among you, this can easily be remedied. Put your clothes and your packs on our horses, and we shall take off our riding boots and walk like you." This proposition was accepted, and after they had eaten and paid the innkeeper, they set out into the forest.

Walter and his servant were carefree and cheerful. But when the three scoundrels thought that they had gone into the woods deep enough for their designs, they quickly attacked the unwary good youths from behind, stripped them of their weapons and their clothes, and tied them to a strong fir tree with ropes. The oldest of the scoundrels advocated killing the two youths so that they could not call for help and be freed, for if the three of them should be caught, they would be in dire straits and might not even get away with their lives. But the younger two refused to follow that advice, for they had some pity for the two youths, and so they said: "Let us be satisfied with this booty and grant them their lives in exchange, for they certainly will be delivered by some merchants traveling this road."

Ah! In what great fear and distress was poor Walter, for he kept worrying that the advice of the oldest one would yet be heeded. "Well then," the old one finally said, "if they are to remain alive, let's not waste any time here, but let's get out of these woods." And thus they hurried off with the two horses.

Then, young Walter began to weep wretchedly and to complain to God about his grief and misery: "Dearest father and mother, if you knew the fear and distress in which I am now, I am afraid that your heart would break. Ah! God! Had I but followed the advice of my father, who exhorted me so earnestly to stay by his side, I would not now be in such great anguish. Oh! You, my dear and faithful servant, should you get no better reward for your services, I shall repent for the rest of my life that you ever came to know me. I no longer fear the thugs who robbed and left us, but I fear that wild animals such as wolves or bears will tear us to pieces with their cruel claws, for even though we have no more valuables to be robbed of, no one coming our way would untie and release us."

Walter continued to lament in this manner for a long time, but his servant comforted him as well as he could, for he was confident that they would be freed.

CHAPTER XXI

🍒 *How Lionel Was on His Way to Lisbon and Arrived at the Above-mentioned Inn. How He Learned from the Innkeeper that Shortly Before Several Merchants Had Entered the Forest on Horseback and on Foot. How He Hastened After Them and Met the Three Thugs.*

After leaving the youths, the three villains rode back toward the inn in a roundabout way so as to cover their tracks.

Now it came to pass that Lionel, whom his master had sent to Lisbon on business, had to ride through those same woods. He came to the same inn where he was told that shortly before his arrival, five merchants with two horses had left to cross the forest. Lionel was well pleased and spurred on his mount with the hope of catching up with the merchants. He had been riding for a little under an hour when the three villains came toward him with the two loaded horses. As soon as they caught sight of Lionel riding alone, the old one said: "Courage, dear brothers, let us attack him all at once; I have good hope that all three of us will be mounted before too long."

Meanwhile, Lionel had drawn near. Expecting no trouble, he

greeted them in a friendly manner and asked if they had not met five people leading two horses. "Yes, and they are not far from you," the old one said, approaching Lionel's horse. Grabbing its bridle, he unsheathed his sword and said: "Dismount at once, or you shall die!"

An undaunted horseman, Lionel did not hesitate long. He whipped out his good sword and cut off the hand holding the bridle so that the old one was no longer able to defend himself from pain and fear. The other two fled with Lionel in hot pursuit, dealing mighty blows. He struck one of them through the shoulder bone. The last one thought to escape through thick brambles, but Lionel pursued him hotly. The fleeing thug became entangled in a thicket, where Lionel thrust his sword into him as far as it would go. The other one lay bleeding so heavily that he had fainted. Lionel dismounted and struck off his head.

The old villain asked for mercy and begged Lionel to spare his life. "You wretched murderer and traitor, you," said Lionel, "you must tell me where you got these horses and what you carry on them." The scoundrel told him everything. Then Lionel bound up his stump with a shirt he tore off one of the dead thugs, mounted up, and had him lead the way. He also took along the two horses. They soon came to the place where Walter and his servant stood tied to the fir tree. The latter feared exceedingly when they caught sight of the old murderer, for they believed he had come back with the sole purpose of taking their lives. As soon as Lionel saw them, his heart was filled with pity, and he hastened to undo their bonds, which had already cut deeply into their flesh. No one could have been happier than the two youths!

Lionel gave them back their clothes and their swords, inquiring into the circumstances which had led them into such dire straits. And when they told him how hard the old thug had called for their lives, and that he had shown no pity for them, Lionel flew into a violent rage against the old man and said: "Since it was through treachery that you enticed these young men to believe your dishonest and false words, and since you had less pity for them than your two dead comrades, you shall receive your just deserts."

He took one of the ropes with which the youths had been bound and hanged the old villain from a branch. Thereupon, they mounted up and decided to ride back to the inn to spend the rest of the day and to refresh themselves with food and drink. Walter and his servant were well satisfied with this. Riding along, they engaged in conversation, and, among other things, Lionel asked about their business and whither they were traveling. "My dear sir," said Walter, with an afflicted voice, "I would have too much to tell you, for I am not in business or in any trade. But I shall tell you everything about myself, my home, my rearing, and especially about my trip as soon as we get to the inn."

Lionel was well satisfied with this answer, and so they spent the rest of their ride conversing lightly until they reached the outskirts of the forest and saw the friendly inn, a sight which caused them no little joy. They were well received by the innkeeper, who recognized them at once. Greatly marveling at their return, he asked for the reason, which they gave him in detail. He felt as much joy as he felt wonder at such news.

Since it was time for the evening meal, the tables were laid. Meanwhile, six more merchants arrived. They came from the kingdom of Galicia and also wanted to ride through the forest and over the pathless mountains. The innkeeper informed them of what had just happened, and they marveled greatly, especially at Lionel's manliness. They rejoiced all the more when they heard that on the next day Lionel was to ride with them across the mountain range.

CHAPTER XXII
❦ How the Evening Meal Was Taken. How Walter Was Questioned by Lionel and How They Finally Recognized Each Other.

The meal was cheerfully begun. Lionel, however, was eager to hear from Walter the reason for his trip; therefore, he started talking to him. "My friend," he said, "pray tell us as you have promised what brought you to this forest."

Walter began, saying, "You may ask of me and my companion whatever you please, and we must satisfy you whenever possible, for today you delivered us from great fear and anguish. So listen, for I shall tell you about myself, my parents, my country, and what drove me to undertake such a trip.

"My parents live in the royal city of Salamanca. My father,

Herman, is a wealthy man who operates a great business by trading with Venice, Brabant, Spain, as well as with many other kingdoms and nations. During my youth, a handsome young boy was reared together with me in my father's house. My father had adopted him while his mother was still nursing him. My parents gave him the same love, food, and clothes as they gave me, their only son."

Lionel understood that this was his dearest brother and companion, but still he did not want to make himself known before he knew exactly how Erik, his father, and Felicia, his mother fared. Therefore he asked, "Dear friend, forgive me if I interrupt you, but pray tell me about the young boy who was reared with you so that I may well satisfy my curiosity."

"I shall tell you everything," said Walter. "Not far from Salamanca there is a village where there lived a poor man named Erik. He had a most lovely wife called Felicia, who bore him many children in great poverty. These were adopted by rich burghers of Salamanca. But nobody offered help or assistance to the good, pious Erik and his wife, and the good man had to make do with the office of village herdsman. These conditions lasted until God blessed him in his poverty.

"One day he was keeping the cattle entrusted to his care, expecting no trouble. But lo, a huge and monstrous lion came among the cattle, and the good man feared exceedingly. The lion, however, harmed neither him nor his cattle but remained very friendly toward him, so that the dogs did not try to chase him away. This continued until news of it reached the city. Many rich burghers and merchants, my father being one of them, decided to witness this miracle. So they would ride out to see the lion every day, bringing him food. In a short time he became very friendly with everyone because of how well he was treated.

"During one of his visits to the herdsman, my father found with him his wife and the lion. Noticing that Felicia was with child, he asked the herdsman if he could be the godfather of the child when God almighty would provide her with the fruit of her womb. The herdsman accepted.

"When the child was born, my dear mother was also present, and since the lion was still living with the herdsman, walking peacefully amidst cattle and people, she suggested that the little child be named Lionel. My parents adopted the child and reared it as I told you earlier. We grew up apace, and my father sent us to school, where Lionel studied so well that he surpassed in learning all of the other boys of his age, and they set him up as their king. In this school, there were also many noble boys, and they elected a king of their own because they were envious of how well we were organized. By and by, a children's war arose between the two kings. Lionel cheerfully exhorted his mates to fight, and so did the other king. Without the knowledge of either of their schoolmasters, they decided upon a good place for battle, met there, and fought. Lionel and his companions took the advantage and prevailed. During the enemy's retreat, they caught a young noble boy whom Lionel ordered beaten with switches. The noble boy greatly resented it and reported it to his father, who went to the schoolmaster to have Lionel punished. He was to receive a good beating, for which he did not care to wait. He thought little more about it but solicited from my father permission to go visit his father. My father gave his permission, but young Lionel had something else in mind.

"He secretly wrote a letter in which he informed my father of why he wanted to go so far away that nobody would ever find him. When I learned about these matters, my heart was sorely grieved, and I decided at that time that as soon as I would reach maturity, I would not fail to search for my dearest brother and companion. Therefore, but a few days ago, I pressed my father to allow me to go on this journey, which he granted with a heavy heart. So I rode forth, hoping—as I still do—to find out, should God lend me his grace, whether my brother and companion is dead or alive."

By now Lionel had heard enough, but he still wished to know how his parents fared. Thus, he asked further, "Good friend, if I may ask, what is your name?"

"Walter is my name," said the youth, "for that is what I am called."

"My dear Walter," said Lionel, "what has since happened to the poor herdsman and his wife? Are they still alive?"

"Yes, certainly," said Walter, "they are well beyond poverty, for my father divided his lands with them, giving them half of all the cattle and of all the crops in the storage houses and barns.

Furthermore, he bequeathed to them the lands as a permanent hereditary tenancy."

When Lionel heard all this, he could no longer hold back the tears in his eyes. Only after he had recaptured some manly spirits did he offer the young Walter his hand and said with a clear voice, "Rejoice, my dearest brother and companion! I am the Lionel you are looking for. Therefore, banish all worries and rejoice with me! Know that after I left your father, I came to the service of a count in the city of Merida, where indeed I fare well. Therefore, I entreat you to ride with me to Lisbon and thence to the court of my gracious count. You will be well taken care of, and I hope also to secure my lord's permission to ride home with you to visit my parents, my dearest godfather, and also your mother."

After Walter had understood Lionel's words, he rejoiced so greatly that he knew not whether he was dead or alive and began to cry from joy. The other merchants marveled greatly at these unexpected events. So they joyfully fell to making merry again for the greatest part of the night. In the morning, they cheerfully made their way through the dark forest and over the rough mountain range.

CHAPTER XXIII

🌡 *How Lionel and His Company Came to Lisbon, and How Walter and Lionel Found at the King's Court the Lion, Who Frolicked with Them as If He Remembered Them.*

They arrived in Lisbon that same evening and took up quarters with a good innkeeper who received them well. The next day, Lionel carried out his orders and then leisurely went to take in the sights of the city with Walter and his servant. They found many costly goods from all parts of the world. By and by, they arrived at the king's court, where Walter found a countryman who had attended school with him and Lionel many years ago. As soon as he caught sight of Walter, he recognized him; he could not remember Lionel, however, for it had been much longer since he had seen him. But Walter was able to fill him in so well that he recognized Lionel, for he had also belonged to his kingdom. When they had become reacquainted, the youth led them to all parts of the royal palace.

There, they beheld many kinds of animals, such as had come from India and Arabia, and at the sight of which Lionel and his companions took great pleasure. After they had seen these things, they were led into a great zoo in which hind and hart, as well as all kinds of animals were wandering about. But among others, they saw a great lion go unbound amidst and amongst the other small animals, at which Lionel greatly marveled. He inquired why the lion was so tame and where it came from, and received answers to all these questions. Walter, who had heard some more about this lion, remarked then, "Actually, Lionel, it seems to me that this may be the same lion your father had adopted."

"Quite true," said their countryman, "I have it from a good source that the king had him brought here from the castle that stands near our city of Salamanca solely because of his tameness."

"Really," said Lionel, "then this lion is the reason why I was named and baptized 'Lionel.' May God grant that my dear father knew that I am so close to his lion!" With these words, he approached the animal and addressed it. "My dear brother," he said, "if you are able to recognize me as well as you did my father, give me your paw." Having said this, he held out his right hand to the lion, which approached peacefully and gave him its paw. The others who were present marveled because they were not used to seeing the lion befriend strangers.

When Lionel and his companions had seen everything at leisure and according to their wishes, they returned to the inn and made merry with their fellow travelers. The next day, Lionel went shopping for his beloved maiden Angeline, for she was always on his mind. He found a suitable present for her and also bought gifts for the maidens in her apartment. When he had been supplied with new letters and had carried out his master's business, he did not wish to stay any longer in Lisbon. He rode homewards the next day along with Walter and his servant, and arrived without trouble in the lands of his lord, the count.

Every day, Angeline had been asking her faithful maiden Florence if she had heard anything about Lionel. She entreated her not to withhold from her anything she would hear about him, and to report it to her as soon as she learned about it. The maiden promised her to do so.

CHAPTER XXIV

🦌 *How Lionel and His Companions Came Home on a Sunday during Mass, When the Count and His Daughter Were in Church. How Lionel and His Companions Went to Church. How the Hunting Dog Noticed Him before Anyone Else.*

Lionel and his companions rode into the castle on a Sunday morning just before the sermon. They stabled their horses and went to attend the service. As soon as Lionel entered the church, the hunting dog noticed him and began to scratch so fiercely at the door of the pew occupied by Angeline and her maidens that they had to let it out of the pews. The dog rushed to Lionel, jumped up at him, and greatly rejoiced at his arrival. Angeline had paid special attention to the hunting dog and was, therefore, the first one among all her maidens to behold Lionel. She heartily rejoiced at his sight.

Every Sunday Angeline and her maidens ate at the count's table, a custom about which Angeline now rejoiced greatly. She beckoned to Florence and whispered in her ear so that none of the other maidens would hear, "Oh Florence, this time you will not get a messenger's reward from me, for I have already seen Lionel." And therewith, she pointed to where the young man was standing.

"Gracious lady," Florence answered cheerfully, "I am happy for your sake that Lionel returned. Now you will be cheerful again. For the whole time he was away, your countenance was as sullen as if you had been gravely ill."

When the service was over, trumpets were blown throughout the court, as was the custom on holidays, since on other days only dinner bells were rung. As the count left church with his retainers, he caught sight of Lionel, who bowed to him becomingly and handed him the writs he had brought for him from the king's capital. The count praised him for his diligence and said to him: "Lionel, you must join me for lunch at my table so that I may hear what happened to you and what you learned on your trip."

The count also noticed Walter, and he asked Lionel right away who this handsome young man was. "Gracious lord," said Lionel, "this is my dear brother. He rode out alone with his servant to search for me, because since the very time I left home, my parents have not heard from me."

"Remember, then, to bring along your brother," said the count, "for I would like to meet him."

When they came to the hall, they rinsed their hands and sat down according to their instructions. After everyone was seated, Angeline and her maidens entered the hall. She was dressed in very comely clothes, and all who gazed upon her compared her not to a human being, but to an angel. But I shall describe her, so that the reader may imagine what she looked like.

She was of becoming height and very well proportioned, her head upright, her hair fair and slightly curled, her small forehead round and broad, adorned with small, brown, slightly curved eyelashes. Her eyes were clear and alert like a falcon's. Her nose was slightly bent and fairly sharp. Her small mouth, not unlike a ruby in color, always displayed a smile. White like ivory were her teeth, small, narrow and set in proper array. Her two chins were set one above the other, a well-proportioned dimple adorning the upper one. Her little neck was round and white as snow, her bosom full and broad, her arms and small hands very well formed, and her hips full and round. All-in-all, she could not have been drawn more delicately by Appeles. Her heart and her soul matched her physical beauty—modest, well-bred, kindly toward everyone, faithful and just.

No less handsome was Lionel; not only did he possess the courage of a lion, he was also kind toward everyone; he furthered justice at all times, hated roguery, enjoyed horsemanship, and was always inclined to serve women and maidens. But above all, he feared God and helped the poor as much as he could, for he never forgot where he came from.

CHAPTER XXV
How Lionel and Walter Ate at the Count's Table and How, in Angeline's Presence, Lionel Told Him What Had Happened with the Three Thugs. How Angeline Listened Carefully.

The count took his place at the table along with his daughter and her maidens, and so did Lionel and Walter. As soon as they had eaten the first morsels, the count began to question Lionel, saying, "My dear servant Lionel, today when I asked you who this young man was, you told me he was your dear brother, if I did not misunderstand you. Should he be, pray tell me what brings him here at this time, and where you ran into him." He was asking those questions because he was afraid that Walter would try to entice Lionel away from him.

Lionel answered the count with well-chosen words. "Gracious lord," he said, "as I told you, my dear brother rode out on adventures, and adventures he found aplenty; he and his servant almost lost their lives. Of this, gracious lord, there is so much to tell that I am afraid I would bore you."

"Dear Lionel," the lord said to him, "let this not worry you and tell me everything that happened to them."

"Gracious lord," said Lionel, "while my brother was riding about the country, yearning to find me, his path led him to a high mountain range covered with a thick forest. On the outskirts of this forest, there is a nice inn in which merchants from foreign countries often assemble to ride through that forest in large numbers, since it is indeed hazardous to ride or wander over that mountain because it is the scene of numerous robberies and murders. In that same inn, my brother found three wicked scoundrels who pretended to be merchants and feigned to be happy, for with him and his servant they would be able to ride safely across the mountains. My brother decided to join company with them.

"Therefore, he and his servant decided not to ride their horses, but loaded these with their clothes, boots, and spurs as well as the thugs' backpacks and went with them on foot. As soon as they arrived at a location suited to their purpose, the three villains robbed my brother and his servant of their weapons; they also stripped them of their clothes and tied them to a tree, debating whether to let them live or not. Finally, they left them and rode off.

"Perchance, I came to that same inn where I was informed by the innkeeper that shortly before five merchants had undertaken to travel through the forest. As soon as I heard this news, I rode after them whip and spur so that I might overtake them, desirous as I was of their company, unsuspecting of what I was to encounter. I had been riding but a short while, when three stalwart villains came toward me with loaded horses. Thinking they were merchants from Lisbon, I addressed them cordially, asking them if they had not seen anyone on their way, but they told me little. The oldest of them, however, threw himself at the bridle of my horse and harshly bid me to dismount and to give him my horse lest he take my life. When I perceived his intentions, I did not hesitate long. I whipped out my good sword and with the first blow cut the villain's hand from his arm so that it remained hanging from the bridle.

"The other two, who had been pressing me hard, took flight. But I rushed after them and slashed the one's shoulder through to the breast. The third one thought to escape me but caught himself in a thicket. I dashed after him and stabbed him with my sword. The one I had wounded was lying in the grass, nearly dead from loss of blood. I dismounted and smote off his head. The one with only one hand left asked for mercy. I bound up his wounds and forced him to tell me from whom they had taken the packs and the horses they were riding. He told me everything they had done so heinously to my brother and his servant. Then, I had him guide me to where they were bound to a fir tree. I loosened their hard bonds and gave them back their clothes, horses, and weapons. But as soon as they gave me to understand that the old villain who was still alive had urged against their lives, I no longer had any pity for him. I took one of the ropes with which my brother had been bound and hanged the old scoundrel.

"After that, we thought that the day was too short to ride through the forest and over the mountain range, so we decided to ride back to the inn. We still had not recognized each other. At the inn, we found several merchants who wanted to ride through the forest with us the next day. Only then did I find out that this was my brother, and what his business was. The following day we came to Lisbon. After I had delivered your grace's letter at the proper place, I went for a stroll with my companions. At the king's court we met a countryman who showed us as much as he could.

"Among other things he showed us a fine and unconfined lion which was quite tame. We were amazed by the mighty animal, for we did not know of his tameness. But the lion came to us at once and greeted me very civilly, offering me his right paw, at the sight of which the other bystanders marveled no little. After

I had learned from our countryman how long that lion had been at the royal court, we concluded that my father had had this lion a long time ago, before it had been requisitioned by the king, and that this was the lion after which my dearest brother's father had named me. This, my gracious lord, is everything that your grace asked from me."

"Indeed, Lionel," said the count, "you report strange things to me. You can really speak of adventures, and I am certain that this lion is a good omen for you. You also proved well enough your leonine disposition with the three thugs. There is one thing, however, which I do not fully understand; you said that you had been named Lionel after the lion by your dear brother's father as if he were not your father too. Do clarify this for me."

"Gracious lord," began Lionel, "I must acknowledge, and not without reason, that we are not true brothers by birth. Walter is the son of a wealthy merchant who adopted me after I was weaned from my mother's milk. My real father was then a poor herdsman in a village, but now, my godfather has bequeathed upon my father much property, so that he is quite well off."

These and other things Lionel told in great detail to his lord, who marveled greatly and was thinking to himself: "This young man will certainly become a man of distinction and attain a high position." Angeline, however, had been taking notice silently and diligently of everything Lionel said, especially as he reported about the three thugs and the lion.

The meal ended cheerfully, and all went back to their quarters or to their business. Lionel took leave of the count, informing him that he had brought back from Lisbon delicate fineries which he wanted to give away in the maidens' apartment. The count kindly gave his permission, and Lionel repaired to his quarters together with his companions. He took out the presents he had brought back and divided them according to what seemed fair to each maiden.

CHAPTER XXVI
❦ *How Lionel Brought His Beloved Maiden a Present from Lisbon and How He Gave Every Maiden in Her Apartment a Pair of Gloves; But How He Gave Florence a Silver Padlock.*

Lionel could not rest until he had given away his presents. He put them into a nice box, which he handed to Walter's servant, and then the three of them repaired to the maidens' apartments and asked to be announced. They were introduced at once, and Angeline greeted them warmly. "Gracious lady," said Lionel, "to show you that I did not forget you or your gracious maidens, I could not help buying a little something for every one of you, in keeping with my fortune, so that, if sooner or later your grace or your maidens undertake a journey, you would not forget me." With these words, he unlocked his box and gave the maiden Angeline her present first. It was a costly coif, preciously wrought and adorned most exquisitely with gold and pearls.

He had given special thought to the maiden Florence, in whom Angeline trusted and confided. To her he gave a costly train, a pair of gloves, and a silver padlock, but to the other maidens he gave only gloves. Such behavior rendered them a little suspicious, and they all thought that Lionel was inflamed with love for Florence. Not in the least did they think that Angeline was the object of his love.

Angeline was the first to thank Lionel warmly for his rich present, and so did the other maidens. Since neither of them knew what Lionel meant by the padlock, they dismissed it from their thoughts. Angeline and Florence, however, gave it much consideration. When Lionel had given out his presents, he wanted to take leave, but Angeline entreated him to stay, for she knew well that her father had allowed him to come to her apartment.

She said, therefore, "Lionel, my dear, I beg you not to leave us so hastily, but to chat with us a little. Tell us how you liked the beautiful maidens in Lisbon. You must have observed them well since you had ample time to do so!" Lionel stood before the maiden, red with shame, for he did not know how to answer such words. Nevertheless, he said, "Gracious lady, since you ask me how I liked the pretty and modest ladies and maidens in Lisbon,

I must tell you in all truth and earnestness that no matter where I wandered and rode, I always found pretty and modest maidens and ladies. But, although I liked some more than others, there is only one to whom I am most partial. I wish to God that my service be agreeable to her; this would be my greatest joy in this passing world."

By now, Florence and Angeline were standing alone with Lionel at the upper end of the hall. Florence was still holding the padlock in her hand, reflecting the sun with it and pondering what was meant by this lock. Angeline, a clever maiden, asked Florence, "How do you like the padlock, Florence? What do you imagine Lionel meant by giving it to you in preference to any other maiden?"

"I am totally at a loss, gracious lady," answered Florence, "but to tell you the truth, it gives me much to think about."

Lionel answered with a smile, "With your permission, gracious lady, I shall resolve these doubts so that Florence no longer need complain. I have presented this padlock to you, noble maiden, because I can well perceive that my gracious lady trusts you in all things above any other maiden. That is why I have brought you this padlock so that you may lock up her confidences safely in your heart."

Angeline laughed becomingly at these words and said, "Well, Florence, you will have to guard the key to that lock with great care lest some false gossip come along and steal what is hidden in your heart."

Florence understood well what was meant by these words and took them to heart. She also decided to keep secret everything Angeline might confide to her.

CHAPTER XXVII
🍎 *How the Count Rode to Lisbon with the Retainers of His Court: What Wonders Came to Pass with the Lion.*

After he had left Lionel, the count thought often of the lion and of everything else that had befallen the youth. He finally made up his mind to see the lion with his own eyes and with Lionel present. Shortly after he had so decided, he was invited to a great wedding, which was to be held in Lisbon. The count, however, did not disclose to Lionel how anxious he was to see the lion, so that Lionel would not be led to think that he had disbelieved the story he had been told. When the time came for everyone to appear at the wedding, the count had all his men wear the same colors and set out riding in great pomp to the wedding in Lisbon. But among his whole retinue, Lionel rode at all times closest to him.

When they came to the aforesaid forest, the old thug with the one hand was still hanging from his tree, whereby the count recognized well that Lionel had told him the truth.

After the wedding in Lisbon had been celebrated quite magnificently, it so happened one day that the count and his retinue were taking a walk in the royal gardens in which there were all kinds of animals. The count still had in mind what Lionel had told him about the lion, and therefore, he inquired very diligently for the lion's whereabouts, which one of the royal servants indicated at once. They repaired speedily to that place and found the lion in a special enclosure. At once it grabbed Lionel with its right paw and endeavored to pull him close most warmly. Lionel began to frolic with the lion, which showed him such friendliness that all the beholders were filled with wonder. The king's steward was also present, and he asked the count who this young man was to whom the lion was taking so well. The count told him all the events that had accompanied Lionel's birth, and how the lion had lived a long time with the boy's father.

This discourse came to the knowledge of the king, who became particularly anxious to see Lionel. Therefore, the young man was taken before the king, who questioned him fully about all that had happened to him since his youth. The king was filled with great wonder and requested that the lion be brought before him. Lionel went at once to the zoo with the zookeeper and enticed the lion to follow him, which it did as readily as a tame dog. Thus, they came before the king, where the lion quite civilly played with Lionel. The king and all those present beheld this with great wonder. He was also taken by Lionel's demeanor. Therefore, he asked the count if the young man could become one of his servants.

"Most gracious lord," said the count to the king, "may your royal majesty know that of my whole retinue this is my very favorite servant. I handle all my business only through him; without him, I would be unable to accomplish anything; everything that I order him to do he carries out quite diligently. Therefore, may my most humble request reach your majesty that you would not bereave me of this my favorite servant." Since the king had a great liking for the count, he let the case rest and did not covet Lionel any longer.

The count's party spent ten more days in Lisbon, amidst great joy, pleasure, and delight. Lionel, however, could not get rid of the lion. No matter where he went, it followed at his heels. And when he was to be locked up again in the zoo at night, he raised a most distressful clamor so that neither the king nor anyone else could find any rest because of it. When told of what caused the disturbance, the king ordered that the lion no longer be locked up but be allowed to go free with Lionel wherever he went. From then on, he stayed in Lionel's room every night.

But when their stay at court was drawing to an end, and everyone wanted to return home, the count ordered the zookeeper to lock up the lion so that it would not follow them. Then it came to pass that he raised a fearful clamor and refused to either eat or drink so that the zookeeper was worried lest the animal perish. He went to inform the king and to ask him what was to be done with the lion. When the king understood the lion's disposition, he ordered his release, adding that even if the animal should follow Lionel home, it was not to be stopped. The lion was freed at once. He did not hesitate but searched out Lionel at once and remained with him from then on. And when later the zookeeper tried to lay his hands upon the animal, he knew how to protect himself.

When the count took leave from the king and sat on horseback with his retinue, the lion was gamboling about in front of them. The king beheld all this and, therefore, told the count to let the lion go with him, for he worried lest it starve to death from grief or become enraged and dangerous if it were locked up again. So, as the lion went forth with them, Lionel was filled with great joy.

CHAPTER XXVIII

How After He Came Home from Lisbon, Lionel Was Sent for by His Most Beloved Maiden: How Greatly She Rejoiced at the Arrival of the Lion.

Within a few days, they were happily back in their own country. Angeline, who kept herself very well informed, learned soon from her most trusted maiden that her dearest friend was back and that he had brought with him the lion about which she had heard so much. Before long, she sent him word that she wished to talk to him and that he was to bring along his favorite companion. When Lionel received this message, he understood quite well what companion the maiden meant. He took along the lion and betook himself to the beautiful garden whereto Angeline had directed him and where she received him with great joy. She had no one with her except the maiden Florence, from whom she no longer kept any secrets.

When Angeline beheld the beautiful big lion, and when she became aware of its great attachment for Lionel, she whispered to Florence: "This sight, my dearest confidante and sister, leads me clearly to think that this young man is endowed with a special grace from God, since from the very time his mother conceived him and bore him under her heart, this lion befriended his father and kept his cattle as tamely as a dog would have done. What makes me wonder most, not to mention the friendliness it showed him in his youth, is the fact that this lion recognized him after so many years, and this alone is proof enough that Lionel and this lion share the same disposition, which was illustrated by the incident with the three thugs. Therefore, dear Florence, you will never again hear anything else from me but that he is well worthy of a queen, and that the greatest of all earthly pleasures for me would be to be betrothed to him."

With these words, she turned toward the young man, saying, "Lionel, my dearest friend, you are no longer unaware of the great love and affection I bear you, and I also have good hope that your first love for me has not abated; should this be so, I desire you to disclose it to me, and also to inform me of how your heart and love are disposed toward me."

Lionel answered the maiden with great joy, saying, "Noble maiden, it would not be possible for me to express either in writing or in words how great and deep is my love for you unless you could see into my heart. However, I must acknowledge that I was born of the lowest parents, and, therefore, it would not become me to disclose to you my disposition completely, since what I desire most can never come to pass."

"You can be quite certain," said Angeline, "that if you desire my person in all honor, this will certainly come to pass. But should you be otherwise disposed toward me, I would completely shut you out of my heart and never again grant you the slightest favor."

"Most gracious lady," answered Lionel thereupon, "far be it from me that I should bear you a wanton love, or suffer anyone on this earth to do so. I would make him pay for it with his life, for my heart and my love are disposed toward you not otherwise than in all modesty and honor. Be assured that there could be no greater joy for me than to be at your service."

"Accept then as a token of my faith that from now on I consider you as my lawful, sole, and lifelong husband," said Angeline. "Neither my father's wealth nor anything else shall prevent me from that! Therefore, accept from me this jewel as a true and indelible sign of true love, loyalty, and friendship."

Lionel was so greatly filled with joy that he could not answer the speech of his maiden. He stood there, quite pale, looking at her until he finally recovered. Then he said, "Oh gracious lady, I never expected this great requital of my love, for I am not worthy of it. But since fortune smiles upon me so graciously, and since likewise your grace is so well disposed toward me, I promise you that from this day on, all my efforts will be directed toward earning the praise and admiration of all men in all tournaments that will be held. I also hope that such actions will carry their rewards."

"By doing this, beloved Lionel," said Angeline, "you would greatly please me."

While the two of them were thus engaged in diverse and friendly discourse, the maiden Florence saw and heard all these things take place; she was deeply distraught and wished in the secret of her heart never to have known Lionel or the maiden; she was afraid that the count might suspect her of having lent them aid and assistance.

Good Florence was, therefore, deeply troubled and worried. Lionel and Angeline, however, were in great joy until the time had come when they had to part. Then they took leave of each other and withdrew to their respective quarters.

CHAPTER XXIX

🍓 *How Florence Worried Greatly that the Love of Her Maiden Be Brought to Light, and How She Chided Her with Words Full of Modesty.*

After Florence had returned to her apartment with Angeline, she began to ponder what had happened, and she pondered more and more as time went on. Angeline noticed the change in her before long. She began, therefore, to question Florence, saying: "Tell me, most dear and trusted among all my maidens, what causes you so much sadness this very day since you have never seen me in greater joy? Don't you know that it is said that one must be sad with the sad, and happy with the happy? Why then don't you rejoice with me since you know that he whom I love more than the whole world loves me too? Weren't you there yourself when I promised him—and he promised me—constant and eternal love? I only took you along so that you might hear of my love and rejoice with me. But you truly annoy me with your dejected disposition and make me think that you mourn because I have taken Lionel as my beloved," concluded Angeline.

Florence heaved a deep sigh from her heart; then she began her answer. "Oh! Lady Angeline! Whatever distrust you harbor toward me does not affect my heart, for it is totally unfounded. I have always used the utmost trust and discretion toward you, but I have never thought that matters would go so far that you would betroth Lionel without the knowledge of your lord and father. This alone is the cause of my sadness.

"And to think that in spite of your numerous messages which I carried to the youth, I never even suspected the great love that was yours! Although I could well perceive the goodwill you bore the youth, I never doubted that this was but on account of the diligent service he performed for you better than any other servant. Otherwise, I would never have continued to carry your messages to him. Bethink yourself, dearest lady, of the great misfortune that would befall me if your lord and father should become aware of my role! I would have to leave the court dishonored! Ah! Poor me! How could I account to my parents for such a shame? I would certainly never be able to face them again. Therefore, dear maiden, my reasons to be sad are not few.

"I wish to God that I had never known Lionel! And, if you should think that the loss of the youth should move me to dejection, you are quite wrong! I never bore him any particular love, but I have not been his enemy either. But since he spent more time than any other servant in your apartment and entertained us oftentimes with his singing and his jesting conversation, I truly enjoyed listening to him, which is why I was always the more willing to call him in whenever you ordered me to do so, especially upon his return from foreign countries. But I never thought that your disposition toward him was any different from mine. Likewise, there is no maiden in your apartment whom I would have believed capable of feeling differently than I did. Therefore, dearest lady, you can decide for yourself whether or not I have legitimate reasons to be sad!"

Angeline was frightened by these words. She worried lest Florence forsake her and no longer further her love. For without Florence, she could not communicate with her beloved, since she could not confide in anyone else at the court.

Therefore, she began to talk to Florence very cordially, saying: "Take comfort, my most trusted Florence, and be rid of all your worries. No misfortune or hardships will ever arise therefrom, since no one on earth—except only you, Lionel, and myself—

bears any knowledge of this love. I have not the least doubt that Lionel will disclose to no one the love and faith which he pledged me, and I to him; the same is true of you. And even if the matter should reach the point where my father became aware of it, I would yet set it forth in such a manner that no suspicion whatsoever would fall upon you. All I beg from you is that you do not break your faith with me and that you give me good advice at all times; also, that you be of good hope and never doubt that I shall be clever enough to bring my father to give me Lionel as a fond husband of his own goodwill and with his blessing."

"May God grant and further your cause," said Florence, "for great would be my joy if it came to pass. But henceforth, dearest maiden, in order to remain all the safer against possible detection by false gossips, you must under no circumstances confide in anyone else on this earth but me—no matter who it may be. Also, to avoid being found out or suspected, you must diligently advise and warn Lionel that he presume not upon your love and favor, but keep showing himself as friendly as usual toward the whole household, and not give grounds for any suspicion. Furthermore, he should not curtail the access which he has always enjoyed to the ladies' apartment, but continue as of old, lest he should arouse the suspicion of some sly gossip. Now that you know that I shall never reveal your secret as long as I live, you must not entrust anyone else but me alone with messages for him."

Thus, the two maidens worked out thorough plans.

CHAPTER XXX

❦ How One Day Walter Accompanied Lionel to Angeline's Apartments; How He Caught Sight of Her Chessboard, and How He Played Chess with Her in the Presence of the Count.

The two lovers lived in great joy for quite a while. Meanwhile, the count grew as fond of Lionel as if he had been his own son. Since the lion still kept him steady company and followed him at all times wherever he went, the count entertained the strangest thoughts about him, and as he could not help thinking about Lionel's wonderful birth, he kept telling himself that it had to have special significance, and that the young man would acquire a great name.

By now, Angeline had already informed Lionel to make sure to visit the ladies' apartment from time to time so that the two of them would not arouse suspicion—as the maiden Florence had advised her.

One day, Lionel went to her apartments with Walter. Angeline, who had been playing chess with her maidens, had left the game on the table. As soon as he caught sight of the board, Walter, who was a past master at that game, told Lionel: "Oh! Brother! My heart and soul are filled with delight when I behold this rich chessboard. Ah! If only fortune would allow me once to play my fill of that game and enjoy myself!"

Angeline overheard Walter's words, and since she fancied that nobody could easily prevail over her in that game, she cheerfully said: "Walter, my dear friend, if you are skilled at that game, let us play a round or two to pass the time and for whatever stakes you wish."

"Gracious lady," said Walter, "I am only a pupil at that game, and therefore, it does not seem right that I play for a stake, for I am afraid that your grace would be too smart for me."

"Never mind," said Angeline, "let us play anyway."

So they sat down at the table. Angeline used every trick she knew, but Walter, a clever youth, ascertained diligently what moves and advantages she needed and let her win the first three games. "Gracious lady," he said then, "if this board does not yield wins as well as losses, I shall infer that I shall never ever learn that game properly. Therefore, let us play the next game for a stake."

"This really pleases me," said Angeline, "and I accept whatever stakes you propose."

Walter wore on his finger an expensive ring. He took it off, saying, "Gracious lady, this ring is the prize. If your grace wins it, you shall have it without any question. But should I win the game, you shall evaluate the ring yourself, and give me its worth as my prize."

Angeline was really pleased with these conditions, for she had not anticipated the ring as a stake. As soon as they began to play, however, Walter put into practice all the cunning and art he had ever learned before, and before Angeline could organize her game, she was checkmated and could no longer move any pieces, at which she sat there red with shame.

Thereupon, the count entered the apartment of his daughter and found the two young men there, Walter, the son of the merchant, as well as his sworn brother, Lionel, playing chess with his daughter. The two youths feared exceedingly. The count noticed it at once and, therefore, addressed them with a smile: "Young men, your presence here pleases me not. I see well that as chess-players you are too smart for my daughter; she could never be skillful enough against you, since two always know more than one! But no matter how it is, I see that my daughter lost this game, for she is hopelessly checkmated.

"Dear daughter," he continued, "if you agree that you lost this game, let us begin a new one; I shall assist you with my advice and stand by you whether you win or lose."

It did not take Angeline long to pick up the pieces and to start a new game against Walter, who applied himself all the more to prevail over the count and his daughter. Thus, they had not been playing long when Walter cleverly gave check to the count and his daughter. The count marveled greatly at such swift moves and began the next game by doubling the stakes. But Walter was quite undaunted; he put to use his art and determination all the more and won every game against the count. Now when the count saw that he was no match for Walter, they all stood up, took leave of Angeline, and cheerfully betook themselves to the evening meal.

The count invited Lionel and Walter to sit at his table, and they partook of the evening meal with great joy, at which others at the court were not a little spiteful; but none of them dared express those thoughts, for they all had been to the wedding in Lisbon and had clearly witnessed how the count had refused to leave Lionel at the king's court when the latter had asked for him. They could easily gather therefrom that the count had set his affection on him. Thus, they kept silent until fortune cast a very bleak look upon Lionel.

CHAPTER XXXI
❦ *How Angeline Gave Lionel a Beautiful Ring with a Precious Stone in the Presence of a Jester Who Was in Her Apartment, and How Their Love Was Revealed.*

Lady Angeline had in her chamber a very entertaining jester, a born fool, whose merriment and sport she often enjoyed. She did not hide anything from her, for she expected no mischief or wickedness from her. But when fickle fortune could not longer bear to stand that the two lovers should carry on with their love so quietly and secretly, it turned completely away from them and caused all kinds of mishaps to engulf them.

One day Angeline bestowed upon her beloved a very fine and costly ring from her finger in the presence of her jester,* neither fancying nor worrying that her secret love would come to light and be revealed thereby. The jester, however, took good notice of everything.

A few days later, a noble maiden from Angeline's apartment was to be married. A merry and splendid wedding was held, at which Angeline and Lionel were also present, together with all of Angeline's maidens. They took along the jester, too. Now when they sat down, Lionel served at table along with the other retainers of the count and waited diligently upon his maiden. The jester also was going from table to table. When she caught sight of Lionel placing a golden tumbler in front of his beloved maiden, she began to laugh, saying, "When will the two of you celebrate like this? You already have the ring, haven't you?" All the maidens perceived these words; Angeline and Lionel blushed deeply with shame, but no more was said on the subject.

Florence, however took it to heart and worried greatly, thinking up ways by which the other maidens might be dissuaded from being suspicious. She used all her talent and diligence to that purpose, but it was all to no avail, for they had understood quite well the words of the jester.

After the wedding was over, Florence secretly repaired to the youth. "Oh Lionel," she said, "how indeed could you reveal your love? For all the maidens who live in the apartment talk of nothing else. Ah! Where were my lady's thoughts that she did not worry about that malicious jester? Now she will no longer desist from what she said, lest she be brought to it by special cunning."

"Dearest maiden," said Lionel, "I beg you in the name of the true friendship which you bear my beloved Angeline, to give me the advice of a loyal friend as to how I might dissuade that base fool."

"Lionel," Florence answered, "you must find the jester when she is alone; entrust to her the ring with a letter and ask her to bring them both to Lady Angeline; tell her that you had the ring sized for her at the goldsmith's, and that you indicate in the letter

---

*This jester is a female, a *Närrin*, as Wickram calls her. To the knowledge of the translator, she is a unique example of a female jester.

how much it costs. Through such a cunning artifice, that malicious jester might be rid of her suspicion. It also would be good if the ring could be delivered at a time when all of Angeline's maidens are gathered and present. Then I shall endeavor to dissuade our companions with clever words, so that none would believe the words of the jester any longer."

This advice was greatly to the young man's liking, and he promised Florence to follow it at once. But he did not fancy that fortune would cross his plan as thoroughly as you will learn shortly.

CHAPTER XXXII

How Lionel Wrote the Letter and How, Together with the Ring, He Took It to the Jester so that She Might Deliver It to Angeline, but How the Jester Misunderstood Everything and Delivered It to the Count.

Lionel wasted no time; he went to his quarters, sat at his writing desk and began to write to his beloved a letter with the following content: "Most gracious and beloved of all maidens, I cannot express either in writing or in words in what great dejection, worry and fright I was cast by the inconsiderate words the malicious jester uttered in front of all your maidens, for the grief it causes me is twofold. I am afraid that our love might be thwarted and impeded by false gossip if her words are circulated and become known at court. For as soon as my gracious lord should hear about them, I would have to fear for my life.

"However, this is the least of my concerns, if I come to think that your father might harbor hard feelings toward you because of me. To prevent this while there is yet time, I follow the advice of your most loyal Florence and return to you the ring that you bestowed upon me. I do this through that hateful jester whom I will lead to believe with cunning words that I had the ring sized for you, and that I am asking you to reimburse me for the cost of the alteration. Therefore, give that useless creature some money and have her bring it to me. As for the ring, keep it until one day fortune brings us together quietly. Hereupon, I wish for you and for myself a time when we might live near each other without fear."

As soon as Lionel had written this letter and had sealed it with his signet, he hastened to search for the jester. She was roving from one end of the city to the other as she was wont to do, and he found her in a merchant's shop, flirting with the apprentices. He addressed her with a smile, pretending he had to call her to court. She followed him very obediently until before the castle, where he believed that no one would see or notice him.

But the count, who was standing on the highest tower of his castle from where he could behold the whole town, espied Lionel with the jester and saw him give her the letter and the ring. Little did he fancy that the letter was directed to his daughter; but he suspected that it might be for some other maiden of his court, and thus he began to talk to himself, "Lionel must be making bold to some maiden from my daughter's apartment, and to win her through that silly jester. I must find out about that, for should he deceive with cunning one of the nobility, or perhaps even one with a great name, there would be much slander against my daughter and me. Well then! I will find out at once!" And so, the count made haste to intercept the jester before she might reach the maidens' apartments.

Lionel thought that he had gone about his case most skillfully, but matters took a turn for the worse, because as soon as the jester had left him, she came face to face with the count who addressed her and asked her what was her business. She answered hastily that she was bringing his daughter one of her rings from the goldsmith's as well as a letter. "Give me these," said the count, "for I am on my way to my daughter." The jester complied at once.

The count recognized the ring at once and saw clearly that it had not been altered at all. He then opened the letter and started to read it. But before he had read much of it, he grew very angry and furious with Lionel. So he went to his apartment and counseled with himself as to how he should handle the case so that he would not cause his daughter to be decried or run into worse danger. He bethought himself very intently of what befell the Duke of Salerno who had young Guiscard murdered because of his daughter, who then followed him into death of her own will by taking poison. At the same time, he also considered the virile deeds and the knightly disposition which Lionel had displayed on several occasions. But even then, he was overcome more by anger than by reason. And so he resolved to have Lionel secretly murdered.

CHAPTER XXXIII
🍎 *How the Count Hired a Wicked Scoundrel to Secretly Kill Lionel during a Hunt and Then Pretend that a Wild Boar Had Slain Him.*

Little rest did the count find, whether in daytime or at night, for he kept pondering about how to dispatch Lionel. Finally, an evil angel suggested to him the following: there was at his court an exceedingly wicked fellow who was also a huntsman and to whom no mischief or disgrace was too much. One day, the count secretly called him to his apartment to broach his malicious plan with him. "My dear servant," he said, "know you that I trust you over any of my other servants, and that I am also full of hope that you will faithfully carry out my intentions.

"Know then that one of my servants ventured to slight me most grievously in my sovereignty, and that I want him direly punished for it. However, I cannot do this myself for several reasons, mainly because my prestige might suffer from it. But in order to achieve the same result with less inconvenience, I am thinking of sending that servant on a hunting trip with you. Then, after you lead him away from the other hunters in the company, promptly dispatch him and announce that a wild boar slew him.

"Should you serve me in this case, you shall be richly rewarded. But I don't want you to tell any man about it, no matter how friendly you are with him. I know you to be man enough to dispatch anyone in such a way that you will not need help. And now, my dear servant, let me know what is your decision and your intention."

The wicked huntsman began and said, "Gracious lord, it would not be any trouble at all for me to venture into even greater perils and danger in your service. One man is no great matter for me, for as long as I have been a huntsman, I have never been afraid of either bear, boar, or stag. And the more spirited they were, the more eager and daring was I to slay them. Therefore, may your grace name and point out to me one or more of those who are a nuisance to you. It will be my pleasure to take care of the matter so that no one will ever know of it."

"So swear it to me," said the count, "so that I may trust you without reservation."

The scoundrel did so at once. Thereupon, the count began, saying, "Know you then that Lionel, whom I loved more than any other of my servants, and whom I elevated at my court, now goes so far as to dare fancy my daughter for his wife, as I have learned through strange ways. He is the one you are to dispatch forthwith and without pity."

Notwithstanding all his malice and wickedness, the base fellow was aghast when he heard the young man named, for he knew quite well how undauntedly he had oftentimes behaved. "Gracious lord," he said, "I don't know of anyone else among all your servants that I would rather not dispatch, for I know well that if he had the least doubt about me, I could not prevail over him in a fight. Therefore, I have to overcome him with cunning. Moreover, he is never seen alone or without having with him Walter, his fellow townsman and sworn brother, although Walter does not frighten me in the least."

The count perceived that the scoundrel was about to repent his boast. Therefore, he strongly encouraged him, saying: "You must not fear Lionel, nor anyone else, but slay just as well whoever takes up his side. Thus you will please me all the more."

Thus, Lionel and his loyal brother were destined to be woefully slain. But they were rescued from their fear and distress by their lion, which never abandoned his companions in distress or anguish.

Now when the count had concluded his deal with the traitor, he dismissed him quietly. But as soon as the huntsman had left him, he thought to himself, "Is it not a pity for such a brave hero, who was never afraid of any man, to be murdered and dispatched without warning by such a scoundrel? How could I ever have thought of committing such an evil deed? Now I would really like to send the young man to the king's court in Lisbon, and give him to understand that should he ever again be seen at my court, he would most certainly be hanged. But this is not sensible either, for should my daughter learn of such matters, she might cause a scandal, and I don't know whether a flame such as hers can ever be extinguished.

"But maybe the youth is born to great fortune, since his birth and his whole life have been so miraculous. Should now such a fortune be destined and provided for him, I could do nothing against it, nor could I ever change it. But then, what would people say if the son of a herdsman should marry my daughter whom so many knights and counts are wooing! For sure, I would be turned to derision and into a laughingstock by everyone. But then, David too was born of a low family, and yet King Saul gave him his daughter as wife. Nowadays, however, the world no longer wishes to think about such matters. Although we all descend from the same parents, there are nevertheless several large estates on earth, and all of them are founded on virtues of which Lionel has not few in him. But be this as it may, he would still deserve death merely for venturing to woo my daughter away from me who had never believed him capable of any malice. Therefore, my first resolve must be followed, no matter what the consequences may be."

Thus, the count deliberated with himself a long time until finally he decided that he himself would dispatch the scoundrel right after he had committed his murder.

CHAPTER XXXIV
❦ *How Lionel Was Secretly Forewarned by a Page to Beware of the Huntsman.*

While the count was thus plotting with the huntsman, he thought that he was alone in his apartment. But there was next to it another room where his armor and his gun were stored. Perchance, a page happened to be in it, cleaning and polishing the armor. He overheard every word the count spoke to the huntsman and to himself. He remained very quiet, however, for he feared the count might discover him and do away with him, too, so that his plan would not revealed. But as soon as the count left his apartment, the page did not waste any time in the other room. He left it in great haste with the firm intention of forewarning young Lionel against the assassin, so that he might find means to alter the course of fate.

He betook himself to the stables in secret and wrote a note which he attached to the mane of Lionel's mount, hoping that the young man would find the message while currying his horse. The note ran thus: "Dear Lionel, your secret love has been exposed. Your lord shall make an attempt upon your life. Be on your guard, and most of all beware of the killer huntsman. I can say no more."

He wrote several such notes, one of which he slid into Lionel's door lock. That same night, when Lionel was trying to unlock it to enter his room, he could not insert his key into it because of the letter. He also had found the other notes, which he had read full of terror. He hastily revealed the whole situation to his brother Walter, who was no less frightened. "Oh Lionel," he said, "I beg you not to hesitate, but let us turn away from here in haste, for should the count have laid such a scheme, you will scarcely escape him."

"True," said Lionel, "as I encountered my lord today, he addressed me very angrily against his custom, and he blushed deeply at my sight. This is enough indication for me that I was not forewarned in vain. In addition, my lord's huntsman never addressed me so kindly ever before. Hence, I must conclude that he will attempt to take my life. Well now! I have been forewarned enough. Therefore, dear Walter, get ready at once, for I'm going to test that scoundrel! Tomorrow morning I shall invite him to ride in the woods with the two of us. Then, I shall trick him into revealing whether he is after my life or not. Should I then have any doubts about him, I shall make sure that he will never again make any attempts on anyone's life!"

Then, the two friends went to bed. The night was a very long one for them. Lionel kept complaining that he had ever come to that count's court, and that Angeline had ever become aware of his services and of his love. Walter, however, was greatly worried lest they would not be able to escape and that they would lose their lives. "Oh Lionel," he said, "even when the infamous thugs left me tied stark naked to a tree, I still had good hopes of returning to my father, but now I fear greatly for you and me, for I am sure that the count must have in store still other schemes, so that if one misses, he can fall back on another."

While they were thus lying in great anguish, they heard a faint knock at their door. Lionel stood up, took his good sword in his hand and asked very softly who it was. He heard a boy's voice answer in a whisper, "Oh dear Lionel, do not leave me outside any longer, for I come for your comfort and fortune. I am the one who warned you so loyally with my notes."

As soon as Lionel perceived his words, he unlocked the door. The boy told them word for word what had gone on between the count and his huntsman. They were a little comforted by this piece of news, since they only had to worry about the huntsman. The boy also pledged to run away with them, for he feared that the count might find out about his warning. Thus, they spent the night together, devising many a plan as to how they should behave the next morning. They also convinced the boy to stay at the court until some other and more auspicious time.

CHAPTER XXXV
How Lionel and Walter Rode into the Woods with the Huntsman: How the Lion Followed Them, and How the Huntsman Hurled a Spear at Lionel but Missed Him.

Now when dawn was at hand, Lionel and his companion readied themselves. They packed as compactly as they could all such valuables as they had, as well as their cash. Thereupon, Lionel went to find the treacherous murderer and invited him in a very kindly and obliging manner to ride with him to the woods, claiming that recently his hunting dog had led him onto the tracks of a stag which had eluded him when nightfall had set in. The huntsman was very pleased by such words, for he was now fully convinced that he would find ample opportunity to perform his vile deed. He told them with a false heart that he was quite willing to oblige them, but that first he wanted to report to his lord so that he would not be punished.

Upon this speech, the scoundrel reported hastily to the count, who was delighted by the news and told the wretch to cheer up. Then the huntsman returned. In the meantime, Lionel had told his companion to set out ahead of him and to wait for him in a certain section of the forest. Lotzman, the lion, had stayed behind with Lionel, as was his custom.

As soon as they reached the forest, the huntsman kept delaying and riding behind Lionel, who would not allow it. As the huntsman noticed this, he trotted a little ahead, upon which he swiftly swerved his horse around and hurled his spear at Lionel with all his might. But Lionel was ready. He gave his steed the spurs, burst into safety, and overran the villain with drawn sword, shouting at him with a loud voice, "Now I have proof enough that you swore to my death, you infamous murderer, you! For that I will give you your just deserts, for today, you shall die by my own hand." Therewith, he delivered his blow with all his might, but the scoundrel put up a strong defense.

As soon as the lion saw the earnestness of the situation, he quite fiercely attacked the murderer's horse and tore it violently to the ground; then, he nimbly brought the murderer underneath his body and smothered him. Walter, who had been waiting close by, heard Lionel's words and immediately hastened toward the clamor. He was informed of everything, while the lion was still crouching on the body of the dead murderer, tearing his flesh from his bones in great anger. In that way, the vile attempt came to an end.

They rode quickly through the forest, taking first the way to Lisbon, and then to their homeland. Walter came to his father's house with his servant, but Lionel installed himself in an inn and went about town for some time without being recognized by anyone except his dearest companion and brother, Walter, and the servant who had been with them.

CHAPTER XXXVI
🍎 *How the Count Was Overcome by Great Repentance When He Heard that His Plan Had Miscarried, and How He Addressed Angeline and Florence with Harsh Words.*

After the count thought that the traitor had fully carried out his order, he cheerfully waited for his return. But when the night came and the murderer had not returned, he became very fearful and worried that Lionel was still alive. "Ah!" he told himself, "how wrong will matters now be! How will things fare if Lionel prevailed over the huntsman and betakes himself to the king, asking for his protection? Then, my evil plans would be discovered! I should have thought beforehand that no one can defeat him, since he has come through so many perils before. Why did I not slay him with my own hands, or give him my daughter as a wife? Who knows, he might have behaved so well and so knightly that I should have held him in great love and esteem.

"But now repentance comes too late. Besides, I have not yet found out from my daughter what relationship existed between her and that young man. Well then! I shall call upon my daughter and her accomplice and find out everything from them; I shall also rebuke them with such words that they shall not hide anything from me."

The count at once repaired to his daughter's chamber with burning eyes and a furious countenance. He addressed her and Florence in a manner which frightened both maidens beyond measure. Then he said, "Angeline, mind you that tomorrow at the first hour, you shall report to my apartments along with your companion Florence, for I have important matters to discuss with you."

Who could have been more frightened than the two maidens! From then on Florence thought secretly, "Woe to us! The jester has delivered Lionel's letter to the count. Ah! How will I fare, poor maiden that I am, for I worry that Lionel has mentioned my name in his writ."

After the count had withdrawn, Angeline, as well as Florence, began to weep woefully, whereby all the other maidens were moved to such pity that they began to lament and to weep, too, although none of them knew the cause of their complaining and weeping.

Angeline recovered first and said in an undaunted voice, wiping the tears from her face: "Oh you, my dearest and my loyal companions, without any doubt, you must have gathered that my lord and father spoke to me in great anger, and he did so to you too, my dearest Florence. But you should not be distraught or frightened, for I am the only one who deserves such treatment. I must also acknowledge something to you: I have loved Lionel, that dear and noble young man, in all faith, modesty, and honor. And worthy of my love he is, for with all his virtue and valiance, he is well worthy that a king's daughter have him.

"Whom did my father praise and commend more often at his court than Lionel? And who has accomplished more brave and valiant deeds than the young man? These are the reasons for which I have to account to my lord and father. May God only grant me to know whether Lionel was slain or sent away by my father. Should he have been slain because of my love, then I shall follow him loyally in grief and pain, for as long as I shall not be able to learn how my beloved one fared, I shall not consume any more food, but mortify my flesh until my soul will not be able to abide in it any longer. But should my father have chased him away from his court, ah! I hope to live long enough to have the joy of seeing him again.

"Therefore, my dear Florence, be you comforted that no harm will befall you because of me. I shall assure my father that you loyally warned me against such a love and that you pleaded against it with the strongest entreaties, pointing out to me all the troubles and worries which now beset me. But I shall also tell him that I was willing to accept and endure all hardships with patience, as I was the only one to know how matters stood with Lionel.

"But I worry that my father let anger overcome him, and that he committed some action which he will greatly repent afterwards. But I, poor troubled soul, must await the hour when I shall learn the truth about Lionel."

As soon as she had thus spoken, she took leave of her maidens and repaired to her chamber. She lay on her bed fully dressed, weeping and lamenting profusely, and wretchedly bewailing and bemoaning the fate of her beloved, for she was convinced that he had been slain by her father. "Oh you, Lionel, most beloved of my heart," she was saying to herself, "if you had to die an unexpected death because of your faith and love for me, I shall always miss you because of your gentleness and comeliness. Why did my father not wreak his revenge upon me and have me put to death in your place, since I bear the greater responsibility?"

Thus, she complained throughout the night, wishing without cease for daylight so that she might learn from her father how

Lionel had fared. Florence's night was no less disturbed. As often as she dozed off, she had one nightmare after the other, until finally, the morning star announced the new day.

CHAPTER XXXVII
🍎 *How Lionel Is Recognized by His Father and Mother as Well as by Herman, the Merchant, and What Great Joy It Caused.*

Now, we shall leave the count and his daughter and relate what great joy beset the good and pious shepherd Erik and his spouse Felicia when they heard that their son had come back alive and healthy, and also that he had become such a tall and handsome young man.

After Walter had been received with great jubilance by his parents, the merchants, they asked him if he had found Lionel. Walter reported everything from beginning to end, namely how he and his servant had been caught by several robbers, were plundered by them, tied naked to a tree, and finally, rescued by Lionel, who was unaware of their identity. He also told them what had taken place at the king's court with the lion, and how the latter was still with Lionel. But he did not reveal that Lionel was already at an inn in the city, for the young man had forbidden him to do so.

The following Sunday, Lionel had his host prepare a fine meal and, together with Walter, decided to invite to it the latter's father and mother as well as the schoolmaster from whom he had taken leave without permission. And so it came to pass.

That Sunday morning Walter came to his father and said: "Dear father, you must know that today I received a message about Lionel from a servant of the king. This same servant kindly invites you to come to him with my mother and the schoolmaster to have breakfast with him, for he has much to tell you about Lionel."

"I am extremely pleased by this," said the merchant, "although I have received a pretty good report about his deeds from you. I shall nevertheless like to hear what he has to tell his schoolmaster." Thereupon, Herman made arrangements with his wife and cheerfully went to the repast. Walter also invited the schoolmaster.

Meanwhile, Lionel had sent to his parent's tenancy a messenger who was to invite them to come hear news about their son Lionel. The good tenant, who had not had any news of his son in such a long time, hastily set out with his wife, and hurried to the inn. Lionel, who had not yet been recognized by anyone, was standing with Herman and his schoolmaster. By now, the first course was already being placed on the table, and they had barely sat down when Erik entered the hall with his wife Felicia and asked for the foreign guest. Lionel was pointed out to them at once, but he acted as if he did not know them. His companion Walter told him, "My friend, these are the parents of your companion Lionel; they come clad according to their custom, for, unlike Lionel, they have little intercourse with the court of counts."

"I am very glad to see them," said Lionel, seating them both. The meal was ended cheerfully, and until the last dishes were brought, everyone talked mostly about Lionel, but no one thought him to be so near. "Ah!" Felicia was saying, "should God grant me to live long enough to see my dearest son, there would be no greater earthly joy for me." Herewith, she began to sigh bitterly and to shed a flood of tears. Lionel was so moved by this sight that he had to rise from the table. He asked to be excused and went to the stables.

Tethered with a chain, the lion was lying on the straw beside Lionel's horse. "Come here, my dear and loyal companion," Lionel told him, "for now I shall show you your first master." Therewith, he unchained him and led him to his guests in the hall. "Now take a good look," he said, "for there is someone at this table whom you know." At once, the lion went to its old master Erik, displaying toward him kindly behavior. Erik recognized him immediately, gazed at him with great joy, and spoke to him.

"In truth, dear friends," roared Herman, "it almost seems to me that Lionel is not far from us, and unless my senses deceive me, he is in this room."

No longer did Lionel choose to hide! He embraced his father, saying, "Hail to you, dearest father! Be comforted, for Lionel, whom you longed to see, is here! And you, dearest mother of my heart, be of good cheer, for now you see Lionel, your son." Then great joy broke loose in the room, and after he had greeted them all most profusely, they sat down again.

Laureta, the merchant's wife, exclaimed, "Ah! My dear Lionel, how could you bear in your heart to detain us so long without making yourself known? You know well that my lord and I love you no less than your natural father and mother here," to which Lionel answered: "I have no doubt about this, but the reason why I did not make myself known earlier is that I was worried that you should still harbor great anger against me because of my secret departure. But since all I perceived in you is love and goodwill, and since even my schoolmaster, who had no little cause to be angry with me, has completely forgiven me, I now rejoice greatly." The rest of the time was spent in great joy, and Lionel stayed several days with his godfather.

CHAPTER XXXVIII

How Angeline and Florence Appeared before the Count, and What He Told Them. How the Count's Servants Found the Huntsman in the Woods, in a Grievous State, All Torn to Pieces.

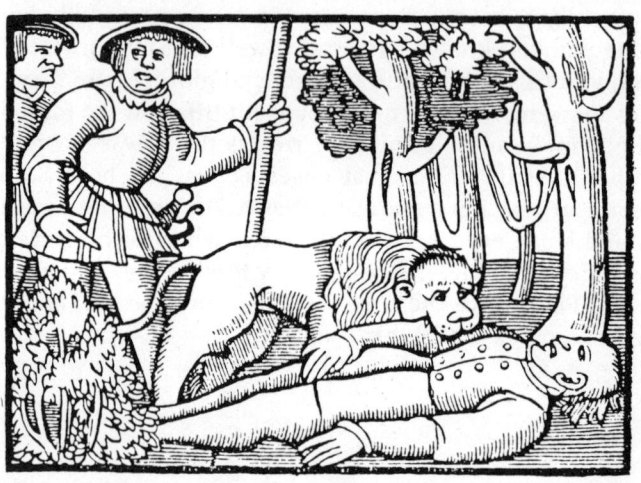

Earlier, you heard how the count summoned his daughter and Florence to this apartment at the first hour of the morning. When that time arrived, they both repaired to his apartment with fearful hearts. By now, the count had already heard from the servants whom he had sent to search for the huntsman that the scoundrel lay in the forest, in a grievous state, all torn to pieces. But they had not been able to determine whether this had been done by a bear or a boar. They had also found his exceedingly frightened horse, running astray in the forest, its bridle torn. The huntsman's spear was stuck straight up in a hedge a good distance away. From these clues, the count could easily picture the turn matters had taken. He dismissed his servants, telling them he had enough information to imagine what had happened to the huntsman.

Now when the servants had left him, Angeline entered with her dear Florence. They bid the count a blessed day, for which he did not thank them, but let fly at his daughter Angeline with snarling words. "Daughter," he said, "why did you not heed your father, but rather deceived and betrayed me so shamefully by fancying a shepherd's son, although one like you could have had a renowned and worthy knight. But now you have belittled my family and my name, and this you will never be able to deny, for I have a letter and a ring which that despicable shepherd's son was sending to you by way of your jester. And it was your fine and dear companion who proposed to that son of a shepherd such a deceitful plan. And the wages which you, Florence, earned for yourself, you can expect in full from me. So this is how you repay the goodness I showed toward you and Lionel! But I have high hopes that the knave has already received his just deserts."

"Oh father," replied Angeline, "it is not possible to vindicate myself toward you, for I must admit that I am the one who chose him, and this I did willingly on account of his virtues and his noble manners, and also because of his knightly disposition; but I have always been so careful that neither shame nor harm would ever befall you or me. And, also, no one at the whole court was able to gather from my actions the love and goodwill I bore him, except my dearest maiden Florence. And as soon as she became aware of my love, she endeavored with great earnestness to dissuade me from it, but she could not sway me in the least. Therefore, dearest lord and father, you must not blame anyone but me alone. I also beg you in the name of all the love and faith which you ever bore me—before you heard of my love for Lionel—not to show any more mercy toward me than you showed him, and if you caused him any pain and suffering, or even killed him, so wreak the same punishment upon me, for should I not be able to find out what happened to him, no human being would ever be able to deter me from following him in steadfast and promised loyalty and friendship, for I shall neither refresh nor strengthen myself with any food or drink, unless I find out what happened to the one who is dearest to me. Cursed be the day on which that despicable jester came into my chamber, for she is the cause of Lionel's losing his life so pitifully.

"I know that the noble young man would have striven to be admitted into the order of chivalry, and that he would have been admitted to it on account of his valiance. Who then would have reproached me if I had solicited him from you as my beloved husband, since you would have found us a good match and would have approved of our promise. For Lionel never did anything else but strive to perform all kinds of manly and valiant deeds so as to earn at all times your esteem, dearest lord and father. And how many times before did this not actually happen, for I heard it so often from you that my love for him increased no little."

All this Angeline said to her father, sighing and weeping so woefully all the while that he gathered clearly that never again would she be happy unless she knew how the youth fared. However, he decided to try something, and, therefore, he said: "Daughter, withdraw with your maiden, and know that your Lionel has not been slain, but is still alive. Where he went, I could not care, but he had better take care not to incur my wrath should he ever return to my court, for he would meet death from my own hand."

Angeline left her father's apartment with great affliction and wringing of hands. She went to her chamber, flung off all her precious jewelry, necklaces and rings, and donned black mourning clothes. Moreover, she would not suffer near her any maiden except Florence and Cordelia. She was visited only by these two maidens who often attempted to deter her from her intent by offering her many and diverse good foods and drink, which, however, she refused to enjoy or even taste. She spent her time with nothing but sad poems, of which she composed several about herself and Lionel, although she did not know yet how he had fared. Now she composed a poem as if her father had sold him on a seagoing ship, and now as if he were in a dungeon, with her sitting every day before its door and wishing to provide him with a prison mate. This was the only endeavor and amusement with which she passed time.

CHAPTER XXXIX
🍎 *How the Count Questioned Cordelia and Florence as to Why His Daughter Remained Shut Up in Her Chamber, and How He Sent for Lionel, Who Absolutely Refused to Come.*

Now that Lionel had disappeared from the court and Angeline neither appeared in her apartments as she used to do nor was seen by anyone anymore, the whole household started to heed the words of the jester. Therefore, there was no little lamenting for Lionel, for he had shown himself so kindly and so gracious toward the whole household that everyone bore him goodwill.

When the count had been duly informed of how Angeline behaved, he betook himself to her apartment the very next day and asked her maidens what she was doing in her chamber since she no longer would leave it. He was told that they had no knowledge thereof, for Angeline admitted to her innermost chamber no one except Cordelia and Florence.

At once, he ordered the two maidens to appear before him in his garden. This took place anon. Florence, still full of fright and with a fearful heart, fell on her knees before the count, and so did the other maiden. He ordered them to stand up again, for he had not sent for them in anger. All he wished to learn from them was how his daughter fared. Cordelia, who had more heart to talk, fell on her knees again and so did Florence. "My most gracious lord," Cordelia said, "should your grace listen to me without getting angry with me, I shall tell you the whole truth."

"Then proceed," said the count, "for I am willing to listen without anger."

"Gracious lord," said Cordelia, "know you then that what bothers the heart of my gracious and dearest maiden is now common knowledge in the whole apartment, for she acknowledged and revealed everything, and unless she finds out what happened to Lionel, she will neither eat nor drink. She passes her time ruefully, weeping and complaining, talking of nothing else but the young man who has completely engrossed and taken possession of her heart. Therefore, gracious lord, should you value your daughter's life and be anxious to preserve it, you will have to let our maiden know about her beloved youth, for all comfort, admonition, punishment, or advice, are of no avail to her. Everything my companion Florence and I have attempted so far has been in vain." While Cordelia was thus speaking to the count, she was indeed crying gently all the time, which he took to heart all the more.

No fewer tears did the loyal Florence shed, her hands clasped together and kneeling behind her companion. The count took note of all this and told the maidens, "Then go back and tell my daughter that the young man is still alive. He fled from my court with his companion and his lion, and he also slew my best huntsman; of this she can be sure. Therefore, she may well cease her complaining and grieving."

The two maidens civilly took leave from the count and quickly brought the maiden Angeline the message from her father; and although she drew some comfort from it, there was still turmoil within her. But she allowed herself to be soothed a little, for the two maidens used all their diligence to that effect.

When the maidens had left the count, he sat in an armchair and reflected deeply upon the whole matter: "Should fortune will it, well then! At least I shall comfort myself that my daughter has chosen herself a mate whom God has highly endowed with virtue and valiance. Ah! If only I could have found out about this long ago! I would certainly have found ways for the king to dub him a knight and endow him with coat-of-arms, shield, and helmet. And then, I would not have been rebuked for what happened, as I am now. If I knew where to find him, I would make haste to send him a message and summon him back to my court."

With such thoughts, the count got up hastily and sent for his messenger, telling him to ready himself forthwith, for he was to ride to Lisbon with post horses. Thereupon, he wrote Lionel a letter and a safe conduct which he gave the messenger, ordering him to hasten to Lisbon by post horses and to ask for Lionel at the king's court. For the count was convinced that his messenger would certainly find Lionel near the king, since the latter had asked for him before. The count also instructed the messenger how he was to entreat Lionel by word of mouth—should his writing be of no avail—assuring him that he would find a very graceful and merciful lord.

The messenger rode off cheerfully, for he had deeply grieved over the young man's departure.

CHAPTER XL
🍎 *How Lionel Stayed in Salamanca, Greatly Afflicted, and How He Daily Went for Walks in the Fields to Lament His Beloved Maiden.*

By now, Lionel had stayed in Salamanca close to ten days. Around people, he hid his grief and pretended great happiness. But as soon as he went to bed at night, he lamented his separation from his beloved maiden from the depth of his heart. Also, he reserved himself an hour or more daily during which he would go for long walks in the fields and sit in a hidden place where he would not be overheard by anyone. Then he would bemoan his predicament. "Oh fortune, how can you be so adverse to me! How can you cross me and weigh me down as you do! You have smiled your false smile upon me on many an occasion and looked my way with your sweet and glittering shine. And whenever I thought to be most agreeable to you, you overwhelmed me with all the bitterness you have.

"Nobody should ever place his faith and hope in you, fickle fortune! You are utterly inconstant, unsteady, and ungrateful, for when one thinks himself closest to you, he is farthest of all. Did you not take wretched me out of a low estate to give me a good start right from birth? And then, after I had been the son of the poorest of shepherds, I was treated quite splendidly. Namely, I was treated no worse than the son of my godfather when I lived in his house, where I was provided with food, drink, and garments quite like his own son. Had you only let me abide in such a position without smiling your false smile upon me!

"But as a young child you wished to make a king of me, which did not last long, for very soon I had to flee from my kingdom, and thus, in a short time, the king became a kitchen apprentice. But still you did not let me abide in that state long: I had to become a servant in the ladies' apartment. And there, Cupid intervened and shot a sharp bolt at me, wounding me in such a manner that I was inflamed most sorely with a burning love for my beloved. And while I was in her service, you looked upon me in such a manner that she and I lived in the hope that our love would remain one and everlasting. But what did you now hold in stock for me with your malicious knavery? Nothing other than that I had to forsake my most beloved maiden without even taking leave. And to make matters worse, I have not the least inkling as to how she fares, although I have no doubt whatsoever that the most beloved maiden of my heart suffers scorn and very harsh treatment because of me and that the whole household is scoffing at her. Ah! Why did I not stay at the court, awaiting my end and death at her father's hand? How can I live without my beloved

Angeline? And how can she trust me now, since by my flight I have left her in dire straits?" These and similar complaints did Lionel utter in countless numbers, and when finally he thought that it was time, he returned to the city.

Before the city, there stood a beautiful linden tree towering above boxwood bushes. One day when Lionel was standing underneath it, gazing at his surroundings, he made out a messenger at a distance, galloping full tilt. As the rider approached, Lionel recognized him as the messenger of his lord, the count. He was somewhat afraid, yet he waited so that he might find out from him how his beloved fared.

CHAPTER XLI
❦ How the Messenger Came to Lionel under the Tall Linden Tree, and How He Cheerfully Handed Him the Count's Letter.

The messenger recognized Lionel before he had quite reached him. He jumped hastily from his horse, pulled the letter from his pocket, and, handing him the count's message, said, "Hail to you, my dear Lionel! I am overjoyed at seeing you. Here is a good message from our lord. Would to God that we were now with him, for he has a great longing for you."

Although he had never known the messenger to be anything but an honest man, Lionel still worried lest the count had bribed him with gifts, as he had done with the huntsman. Therefore, he accepted the letter from him, greeted him in a friendly manner, and said: "Dear messenger, do ride into the city and make your horse fast at the door of the first inn. As soon as I have read this letter, I shall join you there and keep you company." This pleased the messenger, who rode into the city, provided his horse with good fodder, and, thereupon, had the innkeeper prepare him a good meal.

Meanwhile, Lionel was pacing outside the city, reading the letter in which the count exhorted him to return home, promising him total peace and safety. But Lionel kept worrying about possible foul play. He repaired to the house of his godfather, the merchant, and put on a good mail shirt in the event that perhaps the messenger might attempt to murder him unexpectedly and underhandedly at his lord's bidding. In order to impress him, he also took along Walter and his servant, for both knew everything that had taken place. But no one else did he tell anything about his errand.

As soon as he came into the inn, he ordered the innkeeper to lay him a nice table, and to seat him and his company in a separate room, telling him that he would pay and reward him well for his trouble. All this was carried out according to his wishes.

As soon as they sat at the table, Lionel could not longer contain himself. He asked the messenger at once how his most beloved maiden fared, for he had well understood from the letter that her love for him was known to the whole household. The messenger said: "My friend, I have high hopes that she fares very well. Before I rode from the court, I heard from her maiden Cordelia that as soon as she became aware that you had left and incurred the displeasure of her father, she refused to wear jewelry and fine garments, as well as anything that may cause pleasure or joy. She was wearing mourning clothes, taking neither food nor drink until her father sent to her Cordelia along with Florence whom you know well.

"These two brought their lady a message from her father that you had been neither slain nor imprisoned, but that you fled from the court with your brother Walter and the lion without taking leave; the count also promised her at the same time to make every effort to find out where you had gone. Meanwhile, my lord entrusted me with the letter I delivered to you, ordering me in so many words to entreat you most fervently to return with me, for he greatly worries about his daughter.

"Now mark that as soon as he had given me the letter and the safe-conduct, I stole to the maiden Cordelia and told her about my trip and my orders so that Lady Angeline might be comforted by the news. I also tried to see her myself, but to no avail. You can believe these my words, dear Lionel, and I pledge my faith as a sure guarantee of their truth."

Now Lionel knew the messenger to be pious, true, and loyal; he trusted him, therefore, and said: "My friend, tell me who directed you to Salamanca."

"This I found out in Lisbon at the king's court," he said, "for my lord was convinced that I would certainly find you there."

"Dear friend," said Lionel, "what would you advise me to do?

Some time ago, my lord was so bent on killing me that he hired a treacherous assassin for that purpose, so that he might run me through with a spear. Now I am worried that since fortune preserved me from such an accident once, some more trouble is brewing for me, and that my lord may attempt to lure me back to him with enticing words so that he might take out his anger upon me."

"This would cause him great prejudice," answered the messenger, "since you have his safe conduct with his seal. You might leave it at the king's court in Lisbon with your friend Walter, so that, should my lord use violence against you, he would have to account for it most direly before the king."

"Well then!" said Lionel, "let us sleep on this matter tonight. However, you have to be ready tomorrow morning, for I shall also prepare myself, and then, should my dear brother want to travel with me, it would greatly please me."

"My dear brother," replied Walter thereupon, "how could I let you leave me so that I would not know how you fare? I shall undertake and dare this journey with you. But you must not tell my father about it. He would not allow either of us to ride forth, if he knew anything at all about this matter."

And when they had eaten and drunk according to their needs, they went to bed, eagerly looking forward to the coming day.

CHAPTER XLII
🍎 *How the Next Day Lionel Rode toward Lisbon with His Companions and What Plan He and Walter Devised.*

The new day was announced by the cheerful song of the birds. Lionel and his dearest brother Walter had made arrangements on the previous evening to take leave of their father and mother, commending and entrusting to them the lion. And as soon as the morning star stood in the sky, they mounted up and eagerly rode toward Lisbon. On his trip, Lionel gave much thought to what course he was to take. Finally, Walter gave him the advice to remain in Lisbon and write to the count and his daughter that he was still alive and healthy, but that his intentions were not to betake himself to their court before he had performed some honorable deed and had achieved knighthood. Then, he would return with the hope of finding a merciful lord.

This advice was to Lionel's liking, but since he still worried that he might be the victim of some trickery, whereby neither he nor his maiden would benefit, Walter was to deliver the letter. All this Walter promised him to do with all diligence and earnestness, for he was convinced that the count would not raise his hand against him.

What Lionel tried to do, however, was quite different, for he intended to converse with the count and his daughter in person through a singular artifice, or else to suffer great danger therefrom. But he kept this plan secret and mentioned nothing about it to his most trusted brother.

When they had reached Lisbon, Lionel wrote his beloved Angeline a letter bearing the following message: "Greetings, hail, and all health to you, dearest maiden of my heart! I have no way to describe to you what great sorrow my departure from you has brought me; but still, my beloved, I am much more grieved by the disheartening conditions in which I had to abandon you so wretchedly, for as often as I think of the misfortunes which must have overwhelmed you, my heart cries for you, for undoubtedly, I have caused you much grief. Is this the one in whom you placed all your trust, and who left you without even taking leave, he who promised you so often not to forsake you until death and to endure any misfortune with you?

"I also imagined with heavy thoughts what angry, harsh, and punishing words you, my most beloved maiden, must have heard from your father, although I was never used to such from him. Ah! How grievous these must have been to your afflicted heart! And I do not speak of the great shame you must have borne when you thought the whole household was gossiping, saying, 'Look at the mismatch our gracious lady contracted! Now she is yoked to a runaway and fugitive born of base parents! Wherefrom will there come one of high rank to woo her who has refused many a valiant candidate already?' These and similar words, my most beloved, you must have imagined, although they did not actually come to pass, for if the messenger your lord and father sent me has told me the truth, all the retainers of the court had a heartfelt pity for us, except for the treacherous villain who attempted to spear me in the forest, and who received his just deserts for it.

"He would have been successful had I not been warned through the kindness of your father's page, who, being then hidden in the armor room, overheard all that was being planned against me and warned me at night against that malicious assassin. By then, however, there was no more time left to see you, my beloved maiden. But to justify myself: what predicament would I not have placed us in if I had not fled at such a loyal warning, since your lord and father was still consumed with a fiery anger against me? My fate would certainly have been nothing other than death. Where would that have led you then, beloved maiden, if not pining away for the rest of your life, yearning and weeping—if your love for me is such as I am quite sure it is.

"Therefore, beloved, you must not imagine that my feelings toward you are different from what they have always been. You may also be certain that next Sunday I shall be with you in person, to gaze upon your loveliness and further apprise you of my intentions. But I shall appear in disguise, for I shall have made of grey burlap a monk's frock, and have a nice little book bound to look like a prayer book. Thus, you shall come to know what I intend to do next, for it is impossible for me to forsake you. Rest in God's care, most beloved maiden of all."

Lionel sealed this letter with his signet ring. Thereupon, he wrote another letter to the count in which he begged most deeply to be forgiven. He also thanked him most sincerely for his guarantee of safe conduct and informed him that it was his firm intention not to appear before him unless he should have achieved knighthood.

He gave Walter these two letters and, not telling him anything about his plans, begged him most earnestly to carry out his business most diligently. So Walter and his servant, along with the count's messenger, took the shortest way to the count's castle.

CHAPTER XLIII
❦ *How Lionel Had a Monk's Frock and a Long White Fake Beard Made for Himself, Whereupon He Rode to the Forest of the Count and Left His Horse with a Hermit.*

Lionel did not wait long after Walter and the messenger had left; he found a skilled tailor whom he hired to make him a frock and a cape like a monk's, out of ugly, rough, grey burlap. Then he looked for a long fake Venetian beard. When he had completed all his preparations, he rode day and night, for he knew the way well: never did he dismount except to eat or to feed his horse, so that in a short time he came to the great forest that lay near his lord's castle.

In that same forest, there lived a holy hermit, or recluse, or monk, however he may be called. Long ago he had been the favorite retainer of the count's father. A cheerful and bold hero he had been, who had slain a great many in assault and battle. But in time, he had become so plagued and nagged by his conscience that finally he was convinced that he could not achieve salvation unless he withdrew from the world. One day, he came to his lord, his eyes filled with tears, to put before him and bemoan his predicament: how completely he was grieved by his conscience since he realized that he had wronged so many men, slain many more, made widows and orphans, and knew not how to atone for his sins in and against the world; therefore, he had finally resolved to forsake that world and to abide in the wilderness until his death.

Now when the count realized what he wanted, he agreed to it and said to him: "My dear servant, since you are thus minded, I shall offer you my assistance. You certainly know that I own two fine and well endowed abbeys, whose abbots are my good friends. Both abbeys stand in dark and rugged woods. Whichever you should prefer, let me know, and I shall assist you with all my might so that you be accepted as a lay brother."

"Gracious lord," the knight answered, "I thank you most sincerely for your gracious offer. But God forbid that I go into a monastery, for since I intend to flee the world, I would land right in the midst of it! What is life in a cloister nowadays but living in full abundance and voluptuousness, as the very learned Bruno von Bamberg gives us to understand so well in his book *Der Renner*,* in which he examines the various estates of the world. In this book, I read so much about my estate as horseman and courtier that I no longer desire to be a knight or to live at court. But since I am to choose one of the two, I would rather live at court than in a cloister, for I know that at court I would achieve holiness as soon as, if not sooner than, in a cloister. For whenever I lived around monks, I found nothing else in them but envy. Everyone wants to sit at the place of honor, and should one be a procurator or a superior, he thinks of nothing else than about becoming prior or even abbot. Jealousy and hatred are rife among them. To be brief, I shall find in a cloister much of what I want to flee in life.

"But should your grace wish to help me with my undertaking, grant me to pick a place in your vast forest and to build me a little hut as I shall make shift to erect with branches and leaves."

"Well then," said the count, "so pick yourself a suitable spot,

---

*According to Bondzio, the author of *Der Renner* is not Bruno von Bamberg, but Hugo von Trimberg. Jörg Wickram himself treats that same theme of the seven deadly sins in *Die Sieben Hauptlaster der Welt* (the seven deadly sins of the world).

and I shall provide that a small hermitage and a chapel be erected for your immediate needs and your worship. Also, decent food from my court will be brought to you daily." And all this came to pass.

Lionel came to this brother after riding at night under the bright full moon, and it was not far from midnight when he arrived before the shelter. He knocked gently, but the brother could not hear him, for he was still praying in the chapel which stood at some distance in the woods. The shelter itself was leaning against a rock outcropping, out of which sprang a pleasant well.

"I don't want to bother the good brother now," thought Lionel, "but I will ride farther into the woods to the hovels of the charcoal burners. Maybe they have left for their village. Then I would still find stables and hay for my horse so that it will not have to go through the night on an empty stomach." Thus, he trotted gently through the woods. But he had not been riding long when he saw a bright radiance through the trees, at which he marveled greatly. "I am not yet at the hovels of the charcoal burners," he said, "but no matter what fire or light that is, no one could have betrayed me, for no one knows of my plan. But maybe some of my lord's servants are setting up a hunt during the night so that they may start out betimes. What am I to do? There may be several among them who are paid to watch out for me and to murder me. I do not trust any one of them. But then! Be it as it may, I must take that risk!"

CHAPTER XLIV

🍃 *How the Spirit of the Huntsman Came to Lionel and Complained Grievously, Giving Him a Thorough Understanding of the Whole Matter, of What Had Been Devised and Carried Out against Him.*

Lionel took the way straight ahead, leaving it up to his horse to lead him. Now when he came closer to the radiance and the light, his horse began to breathe heavily, to snort, and tremble so much that it was all covered with sweat. Then also the young man perceived such a horror that his hair stood on end. He crossed himself and thought: "I have been exposed to many dangers on land and water, but never have I been so frightened. But be it as it may! I shall continue in the name of God." Just then, his horse started to shy away, paw the ground, and rear on both hind legs. Lionel summoned the courage of a man, spoke valiantly to his steed, spurred it on, and violently charged ahead toward the radiance. Then, he heard a woeful outcry and a plaintive voice, from which he gathered that it was a ghost.

When he had drawn very close to the ghost, it began, saying, "Oh woe is me! Dear Lionel, how hard am I tormented because of you! Woe to me, Lionel, that in all my days I ever ventured to cause you any harm, since no one bore you any ill will except the count. Why did I not let him try his luck with you himself!"

"Poor creature, you," said Lionel, "I don't know who you are, but as far as I am concerned, I do not begrudge you to find your rest." He was so shocked at that sight that he no longer remembered the huntsman who had attempted to murder him. Therefore, he asked very seriously, "Why not tell me who you are, so that I may understand the cause of your predicament and know how you came to such distress."

"Ah! Most blessed Lionel," the ghost answered, "unfortunately, I intended to murder you not long ago because of the presents and gifts which were promised to me. But I did not succeed in this and was killed by your lion. Since I was engaged in such an evil undertaking, and since I forgot to ask God the Almighty for mercy, I must spend eternity in such wretchedness, and no one can deliver me therefrom."

Unaware of what he was doing, Lionel asked the ghost from whom he had received such a promise. The ghost answered thus: "I don't have to tell you such things, Lionel, for you were full well informed of them before; I know who happened to warn you, namely, the page. Otherwise, you would never have suspected anything wrong or amiss!" Not until then did the ghost disappear with great and woeful outcries, beating the flames from him so that Lionel was afraid that the whole forest would catch on fire.

When he saw the moon's radiance shine through the trees once more, he rode on in great fear. "Oh! God," he thought, "now this huntsman must be damned for all eternity since death carried him away in such evil undertaking. How then must fare the many warriors and robbers who set forth for no other purpose than to rob, burn, slay, and make widows and orphans? Ah! How many a one dies or is slain in such a grievous state that he can heed neither God nor his patron saint! And what brings them to do so if not that accursed and vile greed which also led astray this huntsman!

"But what shall I say about the many unfortunates who die at home in their beds and who not only exploited poor people in their days through greed and usury, but who, when attacked by disease, think little of how to minister to their souls so as to achieve eternal bliss! They send at once for a physician wherever he may be so that he may use all his science to keep alive their foul body. But should there come a physician of souls, bringing with him the right kind of medicine and telling the sick man about patience and forgiveness, admonishing him to carry the cross with which he is burdened, he does not want to hear of it at all. He turns his head away from him, asks again about worldly affairs, and starts talking about his possessions, his children, and his servants! Ah! How many a man dies in such a manner, refusing to hear about God! Those are the ones whom God condemns."

With such thoughts, Lionel rode a long time through the forest. Finally, he heard a human voice in the distance, singing and making merry. "I will ride toward these sounds," he thought, "they give me more pleasure than that wretched huntsman did."

He saw the charcoal hovels from a distance and was very glad, for he had found the night very long so far.

CHAPTER XLV
How in the Dark of Night Lionel Came to the Charcoal Burners; How They Talked to Him in a Friendly Manner and Told Him Everything that Was Said about Him.

Lionel reached the charcoal burners. These were working hard, all the while singing, and making merry. He addressed them in a friendly manner, greeted them, and asked them if they could provide him with a shelter for the rest of the night. They received him very kindly and said that if he would make do with what they had, they would do their best. "That suits me well," said Lionel, dismounting. They took his horse, led it to a small hut, gave it barley and hay, and also made it a good litter of straw.

Then they asked Lionel if he were hungry and if he wanted them to bring him some food. He answered that this would please him greatly, and so they brought him good salt meat and bread, as well as a jug of fresh beer. He sat down and ate until he was quite satisfied. Then, he stood around with the charcoal burners, watching them work. One of them, a great wag, asked him from where he came and who had recommended such a good innkeeper. Since he was a good-natured youth, Lionel answered him jokingly, "Certainly, it is up to the innkeeper how he wants to treat me, but to tell the truth, it has been a long time since I have seen a more pleasant innkeeper; besides, the food and drink were quite to my taste."

The one who had addressed him, looked at him often and kept thinking: "This fellow is certainly Lionel for whom the count is asking so eagerly. If I were sure of that, I would earn a good messenger's reward by reporting him to my lord tomorrow."

Lionel noticed this at once and realized what was on his mind. "Without any doubts, this babbler does not gaze at me so sharply for nothing. What if he should report me tomorrow? Then, my present plan would become worse than my last. Let me test him whether he knows me or not." He began and said: "Dear Charcoal Burners, do tell me how long you have been burning coal in this area?"

One of them answered him, "It has been about ten weeks now that we have worked without cease, day and night. None of us has seen a bed other than such as we made right here of leaves from the trees which we carried into our huts. Should such not be good enough for you, you will have to spend the night without sleep."

"I am well accustomed to living it up, as the common expression goes," said Lionel, "and to stay up all night long. But since you have been in the forest for so long, tell me rather if perhaps a young horseman did not come to you, accompanied by another one who was leading a lion with him."

"Certainly not," said the first charcoal burner. "As a matter of fact, I was convinced that you were the youth who always went about my lord's court with a lion. Therefore, I rejoiced, hoping to obtain a goodly reward from my lord if tomorrow I had reported that you were still alive, for there is a great yearning for the young man at court."

"I am well aware of that," said Lionel, "for I am myself one of my gracious lord's servants, and I have been riding many a day in search of Lionel. But all I ever found out about him was three nights ago when I took up quarters with a trustworthy innkeeper who told me in all confidence that one of my gracious lord's postmen had taken quarters with him three and a half days before I had arrived there, and that he had carried a letter from my gracious lord to Lionel in Salamanca, where he is supposed to be with his lion. For sure, the innkeeper heard the messenger say this with his own lips. But whether this be true or not, I shall learn before tomorrow morning nine o'clock."

"Well then," said the charcoal burner, "should I have had to bet all my belongings, I would have done it, so convinced was I that you were Lionel!"

"I am not surprised at all," said Lionel, "for I have been addressed several times in his stead."

Then they changed the subject and chatted away the rest of the night. Lionel helped them stack up and carry wood so that the night would be so much shorter for him. But as soon as the night was over and day broke, he gave them a gratuity, for which they thanked him warmly. Then he mounted his horse, took leave of the charcoal burners, and rode back to the hermit's hut.

CHAPTER XLVI
🍎 *How in the Morning Lionel Found the Hermit Sitting before His Shelter; How the Brother Received Him.*

Great indeed was Lionel's desire to find the monk. He knew him very well and was convinced that he would not be turned away by him. Now when he came to the shelter, he found the brother sitting in a pleasant spot close to a well. He greeted him kindly and for a little while remained still on his horse. The brother thanked him, gazed at him earnestly and marveled at his coming, since he had heard from several retainers of the court that he had ridden off and no one knew where he could be found.

But after he had fully recognized him, he cried out: "Lionel, my dear friend, is it you, or does my sight deceive me? I cannot believe that you make so bold as to ride into the lands of my gracious lord after what I heard! But should you be Lionel—as I believe you are—then I beg you to forsake these lands in haste. I worry that unless my lord be disposed differently than one month ago, you would not stay alive should he lay his eyes on you."

Lionel pulled out the safe-conduct which the count had sent him in secret and said: "Richard, dear brother, pray read this safe-conduct my lord had sent and delivered to me in Salamanca."

"I rejoice from the bottom of my heart about this," said Richard as soon as he had read the letter, "for your departure grieved me greatly. But now tell me, have you already been at court, or is it your intention to go there now?"

"I have not made up my mind yet, dear brother Richard, and therefore, I come to solicit your advice."

"I am at a loss as to give you any advice in this case," said the brother, "but should I fathom the mind and disposition of the present lord as well as I did that of his long-deceased father, I would know quite well what to tell you, for he held very loyally to what he promised and agreed to; but then, I have never heard anything else about this one. Moreover, you have been around my gracious lord all your youth, so that you should know him much better than I do."

"As a matter of fact," said Lionel, "I have never seen him use violence against anyone, but I have known him at all times to be of a gentle and mild disposition. Still, I do not want to expose myself too openly before I have spoken in person to my beloved maiden, as I shall attempt to do.

"Know you, my dear brother, that in Lisbon I secretly had made a habit, a cape, and a coat, and also a fake beard, so that I may disguise myself as a monk. I have also written to my beloved maiden by way of my dear and trusted brother Walter in Salamanca that this Sunday I would go to her church, and that she would be able to see me there, at the entrance of it in the guise of a monk and speak to me in person. I shall give her with my own hand a beautiful booklet in which she will find an account of my birth and of my whole life up to the present times, as well as what I further intend to do or lose my life doing, namely, that I shall seek service at the king's court and curry favor of the king in such a manner that I hope to be dubbed a knight before long, so that her father would not think only of my birth, but also of my worthy and manly deeds."

"Lionel, my dear friend," said the hermit, "should these be your intentions, you will have to proceed prudently lest the same fate befalls the book as did the ring and letter that, when you thought to convey them to the maiden, fell into her father's hands. I know of this through a page who daily brings me my food from the court; that same one also told me during confession how he was the cause of your being alive by warning you against the treacherous hunter."

"Ah God!" cried Lionel, "would I like to see that boy! He would be my righthand man for my whole undertaking."

"Be certain of that," said Richard, "for unless he passed away this very night, he will be with me in this wood before two hours are up. You would do well to consider what you want to tell him."

Lionel said: "My dear Richard, what did the boy tell you the last two days? Did he not see my brother at court?"

"No, not at all," said Richard, "for indeed we have not talked about you for three days."

"I am quite convinced that my companion is at court by now," said Lionel.

Thus they spent their time, happily conversing with each other until the time when the boy was to come with the food.

CHAPTER XLVII
🌿 *How the Page Came with the Food, and What Great Joy Overcame Him When He Saw Lionel.*

There was in the forest, at about a stone's throw from Richard's shelter, a tall and smooth stone column. Every day, the brother's food was brought there by the page or someone else from the court. The upper part of that column was hollowed out like a box and could be covered by a flat stone so that the birds and other wild animals would not steal the brother's food in his absence. It had also been ordered that, should the brother not be found at the rock, whoever was bringing the food would put the victuals in it and then return to the castle. Often the brother left it untouched for several days. Then, whoever brought him his food and found the old meal still in the stone, simply replaced it with the fresh one. Thus the brother would not be disturbed during his devotions and prayers.

Richard and his visitor betook themselves to that stone. Lionel was wearing his cape so that he would not be recognized should anyone other than the page bring the food. They had not been waiting long when the boy arrived with the food. Richard received him kindly as he always did and asked him what new tidings there were at court. "I have very good news," said the boy, "a few days ago, a letter came to my lord from our dear Lionel, who is now believed to be at the king's court in Lisbon. His sworn brother Walter told me so himself."

"Ah! My dear son," said Richard, "no matter who told you so, I tell you in all truth that he is not in Lisbon, and that nobody there knows where he is. I was well informed of that, for as soon as Walter and the messenger rode out of Lisbon, Lionel disappeared from the court."

"Ah! May God have mercy," said the boy. "I worry that he was taken prisoner or even died through some foul deed my lord may have carried out against him," and he began to weep most wretchedly.

Now when Richard and Lionel had thus ascertained his loyalty, the brother continued, "I told you the whole truth, dear son, and to prove it, here is Lionel." Therewith, he pulled back Lionel's cape. The boy was so filled with joy that he could not stay on his horse. He jumped down at once and greeted Lionel with great joy, saying, "Oh Lionel, should now my gracious lady know that you are so close, I am sure that she would faint from joy, for it is impossible to express in words how much she longs for you. But now her sorrow has already partly turned to comfort. For as soon as your brother Walter came to my gracious lord, and my lord read your letter, he had Walter himself take it to his daughter so that she would be convinced beyond the shadow of a doubt that you are still alive. Walter also informed my gracious lady of many things, among others how during the night I warned you against the murderous traitor, for which my lady began at once to show me much kindness.

"Today the whole household is rejoicing greatly; the ladies in the apartment are now filled with delight since they know you to be alive and healthy, for the whole host of us felt great sorrow and grief because of you. But now they all know that you fare well."

Lionel rejoiced greatly at these words, and only now did he fully trust the writ the count had sent him. However, he abided by his decision not to live at the court of the count until he had served some time at that of the king. He begged the boy most urgently not to inform Walter or anyone else of his presence so that his undertaking might take its course unhampered. The boy promised him this, and since it seemed time, remounted and rode back to court, for it was just about the time when the dinner bell would be rung, as was the custom at court.

CHAPTER XLVIII

🍎 *How that Sunday Lionel Waited in Front of the Church; How Angeline Recognized Him at Once and Ordered that He Be Given Alms.*

That Sunday, Lionel wrapped himself up in his cape and habit, donned his long beard, and took the shortest way to the court. In one hand, he held a thick prayer book, and in the other a small crucifix mounted on a staff. Upon reaching the gates of the outer court, he was admitted without any ado, for the gatekeeper believed him to be Richard, the hermit. Lionel took up his stand in the outer court at the entrance of the church and waited for the people to come. At the appointed time, the retainers arrived in due order, one after the other.

The count did not go to church that day, for he did not feel quite well. But Angeline could hardly await the hour. She dressed herself most magnificently and ordered all her maidens to don their festive attire, wherefore there arose among them the suspicion that Lionel might come to court, but none of them knew quite how he was to carry out his plan, except Florence and Cordelia, to whom Angeline had told the whole matter.

Now when the bells were rung for mass, Angeline and the

maidens of her apartment set forth in such splendid array that they looked like a host of angels sweeping by. As soon as they reached the church, Angeline caught sight of the brother, who came toward her with great reverence. At once she gave him a costly present as well as a pair of gloves in which she had hidden a letter and said: "Pray remember me for these alms, brother."

"Have no doubts about that, gracious lady! In return, I beg you to accept from me with good grace this prayer book, and to read it with diligence, for it contains something you will really like."

Lady Angeline accepted the book from the brother and ordered the closest of her maidens, Florence, to take good care of it. Florence and Cordelia, however, who could not approach the brother, let him know by signs that they had recognized him. The rest of the maidens wondered about the brother, who he was or where he came from to be given so much attention by Lady Angeline. But among the rest of the household the rumor was that Brother Richard had come to court from the forest. When mass was over, and the dinner bell was rung, everyone left church. The page drew Florence aside and said: "Ah, gracious lady, would you lend me your patronage so that I may get the good brother some fine morsel from the kitchen? For I know him quite well, and not so long ago, I knew him under better circumstances."

The maiden understood quite well what the boy meant, and, therefore, she said: "My boy, go to the kitchen and tell the cook to give you good food, and plenty of it, both for yourself and the brother. Then take him to a guard-room and entertain him. Come to my chamber after the meal, and I shall tell you a story that you are to tell the brother to shorten his time in the forest." All this was carried out according to her orders.

When Lionel had eaten his meal, he asked the boy to tell him Florence's story the next morning, whereupon he returned to the forest, filled with great joy. He read the letter he had received from Angeline, in which she recommended to him most warmly the page, since it was his warning that had saved him from death. Among other things, she informed him also how highly the count regarded Walter. Then, she begged him that if he were to leave again, he should come to the court once more in his disguise so that her father could see him, since such a visit also might entail much good for him. All this, Angeline did very craftily, for she hoped thereby to retain Lionel at the court. But it was of no avail, for he wanted to comply with what he had promised the count in writing.

CHAPTER XLIX
❦ How Angeline Sent for Walter and Revealed to Him Everything about Lionel's Presence and How She Had Spoken to Him in Person.

By now, while Lionel was back in the forest with his friend and trusty brother, Angeline was pondering intently by what means she might bring Lionel to give up his undertaking so that he would stay at court and not ride away again, for the thought of his departure filled her with grief. As soon as she got up from the table, she sent for Walter. He heeded the lady's order forthwith and repaired to her in a hurry. She received him in a friendly manner and with great joy, saying to him with a smile, "Oh Walter, had you been with me today, you could have seen your brother Lionel in person, and you could have spoken to him."

"Gracious lady!" said Walter, "I have not the slightest idea of what you mean, for I neither believe nor think that Lionel would come so close and conceal himself from me, for should such have happened, I would be not a little vexed."

Thereupon, Angeline answered: "You must not think in any way, my dear Walter, that it happened in distrust or suspicion. When Lionel spoke to me, his appearance was concealed under a disguise, for he spoke to me in front of all my maidens, but none of them recognized him. Today, he was at the court dressed as a monk. Now if he acted so secretly toward you, it was because he was afraid that you would have been either so frightened or so pleased that your behavior would have given him away. But he wrote me earnestly that tomorrow you are to go to him with the page, for the boy knows well where your brother presently stays, namely with hermit Richard in the forest."

When Walter heard this from the maiden, his hair stood on end from fear, although he no longer worried as far as the count was concerned, for, being with him daily, he had noticed nothing that suggested the count bore Lionel anything but goodwill and kindly feelings. However, he worried lest the count should discover that Lionel had been at court under a disguise, although he had rejected his written invitation. This the count might take in bad part and with anger, and perhaps even think that Lionel had planned some underhanded trick against him. "Oh, gracious lady," he said therefore, "since Lionel decided to come here, why did he not ride with us, since my gracious lord wrote him in such a friendly manner and granted him safe conduct? Ah! What can be on his mind? With his way of acting, my lord may also come to suspect me of having dishonorable intentions."

"Never mind, dear Walter," said Angeline thereupon, "for I have in mind a plan that will restore peace and comfort to all of us if only you and Lionel will heed my advice. But above all else, you must see Lionel and tell him not to leave without having seen my father."

With her permission, Walter took leave from Lady Angeline, promising to visit Lionel in the forest on the morrow. He found the page with whom he made arrangements so that the next day the two of them could ride to Lionel without any other company.

CHAPTER L
🍂 *How in the Morning the Page and Walter Came to Lionel in the Woods; How They Spoke to Each Other.*

As soon as the page learned from Walter that Angeline had disclosed the whole matter to him, he was satisfied, and promptly started gathering enough food and drink for Richard and Lionel so that the next morning they could ride to the forest all the earlier. Now when they had made all their arrangements, they went to bed and slept without worries. The next morning, as soon as the doors were opened at the crack of dawn, they rode hastily to the forest. Richard they found praying in his shelter, but Lionel was still sleeping in a heap of grass and leaves he had gathered for himself. Walter went to him at once and kicked him in the ribs, saying, "It does not become a hermit to sleep so late; he should be praying long since!"

Lionel recognized the voice of his companion at once. He started, full of shame, but also fright at the thought that Walter knew about his secret undertaking. "Oh Walter," he cried out very humbly, "my dearest brother, I beg you not to hold it against me that I acted so secretively and surreptitiously toward you, for truly I was not motivated by distrust, since I never perceived anything but friendship and brotherly loyalty in you! But I did this only because I worried lest you would never allow me to carry out my undertaking, should you have known about it beforehand. I also know that should you have recognized me last Sunday as you passed by me along with the other servants of the court, you would have been worrying and fearing for me beyond measure. Therefore, I did not want to distress you. But now I beg you cordially to tell me who told you about me."

"Actually," answered Walter, "I have been quite distressed because of you. But I cannot understand how I deserved your acting so secretively toward me. I still would be ignorant of your presence had not Angeline told me so yesterday. Did you not worry that someone might report you to the count? What do you think that he would have inferred from your behavior, if not that you had hidden designs against him? And then myself, innocent as I was, I would also have had to suffer, since I brought him your letters, which your present behavior calls into question, nay which, if anything, makes it look as if we were about to carry out some foul deed. Therefore, I have sore grievances against you.

"Also, you shall never again set me at rest unless you make yourself known to the count. Should you still bear me your old loyalty and friendship, then grant me one thing that I shall request and beg from you, namely, the one thing which Angeline requests from you also: come to the court in your monk's habit and make yourself known to the count by speaking to him in person. Thus, all his suspicions would be allayed."

"That does not suit me at all," cried Lionel, "for even if my lord no longer hates me, and if, according to his writ, he has forgiven me, I still have to live up to the letter I sent him."

"You certainly lived up to it in a fine way indeed by going to his court last Sunday and by talking with Angeline in person!" said Walter thereupon. "How will you explain that to the count if he discovers it? And now you have no reason whatsoever to worry about him; I have been around him every day since I delivered your letter, and I have had to sit with him at table at all times, and not one meal was served at which he did not remember you in a most friendly manner; moreover, he has in mind to send me to Lisbon. But should you want to live up to your promise completely, you would repair to the count in your disguise, and earnestly beg him for forgiveness. Then you should apprise him in your own words of your intentions. Thereby, he will be convinced beyond doubt that you do not distrust him any longer but give credence to his writ. Then, point out to him that you donned this strange habit to be able to speak to him in person without being recognized by any of his retainers. This would certainly impress him very favorably and enable you to live at the king's court with more joy and peace of mind."

Lionel liked this piece of advice well and decided to follow it. However, he said: "Walter, I shall follow your advice, but on the condition that you first announce my arrival to the count, and at the same time, observe very diligently his reactions, what color his face turns, how his eyes shine in his head, whether he clenches his teeth or not, or becomes restless. Should he answer you with an angry heart, and should his face turn red as fire and white right afterwards, it is a sign of hidden anger. Or else, should his eyes roll to and fro in his head, or should he stagger on his feet and should his hands shake, you can be sure that he harbors against me an anger as strong as ever. Should you notice these signs in him, you are not to waste any time at court, but at once ride out to me with your servant. Then we shall set out at night and ride off. The moon is presently full, and I know of ways and roads on which nobody will be able to follow us. Thus, we shall be able to leave these lands without becoming lost."

The two youths agreed on this plan. Walter rode back to the court, and as soon as the opportunity arose, he repaired to the count, telling him everything Lionel had asked him to say. He also paid diligent attention to whether he could discern any signs of anger in him. But no anger was left, nothing but joy, for as soon as the count heard that Lionel was to come to his court the next day, he ordered a delicious meal to be prepared, and he also announced the news to his daughter Angeline, for he still did not know that Lionel had been at court. Now when Walter sensed such goodwill in the count, he at once sent the page to Lionel with the message that he need not hesitate to come to the court the next morning, since the whole matter stood well and good. When Lionel heard this, he was in high spirits and awaited with joy the next day when he would again see his beloved Angeline.

CHAPTER LI
How Lionel Came to the Count in His Monk's Habit, and How the Count Took Him to His Apartment.

The next morning, Lionel got up and took leave of his brotherly companion, the hermit, who wished him good luck for his undertaking, and also that he might find a merciful lord. Then Lionel set forth in a hurry and came to the castle gates before they were open. He sat before them until they were open, and then he went straight to the church to wait for his brother Walter, for that was where they had agreed to meet. Before long, Walter arrived with the page, full of joy. Walter told him everything he had heard from the count, wherefrom Lionel gained no little comfort.

By that time, the count had awakened and was getting dressed. Thereupon, he lay in a window of his apartment and listened to the song of the birds, which he greatly enjoyed. When the page caught sight of the count at his window, he announced it to the two youths. Walter did not waste any time; he repaired to the apartment of the count and knocked very cautiously. The valet opened the door to the antechamber at once and asked him what his business was. "Should my lord be up," Walter said, "please announce me, for I have an urgent matter to report to him." The boy did so.

As soon as he laid his eyes upon Walter, the count fancied that Lionel had arrived. Walter bowed to him and wished him a blissful morning. The count thanked him cordially and asked him, "Walter, what does your early call mean? Tell me, is there anything new?"

"Gracious lord," said Walter, "the monk about whom I told you yesterday is already here."

"I'm glad to hear this," said the count. "But tell me, Walter, where is he?"

"Gracious lord," said Walter, "he is sitting in the church, waiting for whatever instructions your grace will give him."

"So go," said the count, "and tell him to meet me in the garden at the postern entrance to my apartment. There we shall be able to converse at our leisure."

"I shall do this at once," said Walter and hurried to acquaint Lionel with the order of the count.

Lionel immediately betook himself to the garden. There he found his lord all by himself and without servant. He flung himself at his feet, crying, "Ah! Dear and gracious lord of mine, the poor servant that I am begs you in God's name to forgive him, for he has deeply offended you."

"Stand up, Lionel, and be comforted," said the count. "I forgive you everything you may ever have done against me, although I never expected any such thing from you. But since fortune is so well disposed toward you, I shall never be able to cross her. I realize that no human device can prevail against the will of the Almighty. Therefore, I completely forgo any such attempt and shall consider no matter more urgent than to devise ways by which I can avoid being rebuked by other knights and counts. Thus, my first and best advice would be that you betake yourself to the king's court and explain that you incurred my displeasure. Since I know the king to be so favorably and graciously disposed toward you, he will not fail to write me at once that I am to restore you my favor. Then I shall be able to justify myself against anyone by saying that the king forced my hand, and that I could never afford to incur his wrath. Should you know of a more appropriate and suitable way, do let me know of it."

"Gracious lord," said Lionel, "I beg your grace not to take it amiss or begrudge my speaking out. I have completely made up my mind to serve the king for a while so that I might gather practice and experience in knightly deeds. I have been informed by several of the king's servants that the king is mustering horseguards to send to the king of Castile, who is being invaded forcibly by the king of Galicia. Should this enlistment proceed, it would be the perfect opportunity for me to become a horseguard. By being quite mettlesome in combat, I would acquire no little honor and fame, which is my ultimate purpose, will, and intention; and I shall have no rest, whether day or night, until my will has sufficiently prevailed. Therewith, I shall guard myself against slander so that no envious one may be able to say: 'What action did Lionel see? In which skirmish or battle has he been to brag so much?' To prevent this, I know of no more certain way than the one I have told your grace."

Lionel's words pleased the count beyond measure. Moreover, he promised the young man to furnish him with horse and armor, and also to give him a squire to improve his chances of being appointed by the king. When they had been together in the garden for about two hours in that manner, the count took Lionel to his apartment, gave him new clothes, and ordered him to take off his burlap. Before doing so, however, Lionel informed him in great detail why he had been wearing such a disguise.

CHAPTER LII
❦ *How Lionel Went to Lunch with the Count, Whereat the Whole Household Marveled Greatly.*

Now after Lionel and the count had conferred at great length, it was time for lunch, and the bells were sounded. Many came to eat, and everyone sat at his prescribed table. But the count took Lionel and Walter with him into the great hall, at which the whole household marveled greatly, for no one knew how or when Lionel had arrived. No one among the household begrudged him that fortune, however, but rejoiced greatly about his arrival.

After they had performed their ablutions and had taken places at the table, the food was served, and the meal took its course mirthfully and cheerfully, and already all of Lionel's ill humor had disappeared; all he lacked now was having his beloved Angeline at the table with him. In no way, however, did he act as if it were so, but he showed himself of quite a happy mood and countenance. With no less joy did Walter see his dearest brother and companion sit at the table of his lord, since shortly before he had deemed such quite impossible.

They were not yet halfway through the meal when a messenger from the king arrived, riding full tilt. As soon as his feet touched the ground, he hurried into the great hall and delivered a letter to the count. It instructed the count to appear promptly at the king's court within thirteen days, and to be supplied with everything he would need for a most pressing emergency, namely, as good armor and military equipment as possible, for the king had in mind to put him in charge of his horseguards. "Upon my faith, Lionel," cried the count, "it seems to me that we have a war at our door. You no longer need to wish for it. I think we shall all get our fill of it."

"I rejoice with my whole heart," said Lionel, "for my very heart tells me that we shall be quite successful in that war."

Lady Angeline had no knowledge whatsoever that Lionel was sitting at her father's table. The page would have liked to inform her of this, but could not leave the table. However, as soon as the meal ended and the table was cleared, he went to the lady in great transport and asked her for a messenger's reward, informing her of everything that had taken place. Her heart leaped with unbounded joy, and she gave the boy a reward which put him in good spirits indeed. Then she posted herself at a window under which she knew that her father would pass with the young man, as indeed they did shortly thereafter.

Around and about her stood her maidens, closest of all Florence and Cordelia. Now when Angeline caught sight of the count leaving the hall with his retainers and Lionel at his side, she said: "Tell me, dear Florence, who is that handsome young man coming out of the hall with my father?"

Florence, who had not been aware of him, saw him only now. She blushed deeply from joy and said: "Dear lady, there was never a more fortunate one on earth than you are this very moment, for you can be quite certain that Lionel is back in your lord and father's favor. You don't need any one to comfort you anymore since now your comforter is back in favor and can stay at court without any worries."

"Now I would like to know," said Angeline, "how the matter came about, and who managed these things so promptly, for I know that on Sunday past, Lionel was not yet so minded, or he would never have had to disguise himself in that ugly habit. Well then! Let me go and find out these matters from Walter."

CHAPTER LIII
🍂 How Angeline Went for a Stroll in the Garden with Her Maidens; How the Count Also Came into the Garden with Lionel and Walter; How the Count Had His Daughter Read the Letter He Had Received from the King.

Angeline kept asking herself how she might manage to reach Lionel in a seemly manner. Taking with her Florence and Cordelia, her two dearest maidens, she went out into the garden through the postern of her apartment, for she knew well that before long her father would bend his steps to the garden as was his custom.

As soon as the count caught sight of his daughter, he turned toward Lionel and his companion and said with a smile: "Well, Lionel! You must have a good messenger for you to be announced so quickly."

Blushing deeply with embarrassment, Lionel answered the count, saying, "Gracious lord, I certainly know of nothing."

By then the count had reached his daughter. "Angeline," he said, "you are really of a clever understanding, for I was just about to send Walter for you and here you are in the garden before I am. But I cannot keep from you this message from the king. Therefore, you may read this letter for yourself and then tell me what you think about his request."

Angeline took the letter from her father and read it to the end; she was so downcast that she began to weep quite wretchedly, since it was no secret to her that her father was a man well advanced in years and no longer accustomed to war, but used to a good and peaceful life. Moreover, she knew that nothing would be able to deter Lionel from taking the field with him. Therefore, her worries and grief were twofold.

"Dear daughter," said the count, "do share with me your good and candid advice. You know what I am made of: my young and carefree days are gone; I grow no stronger, but weaker apace, for I am far past my prime. But still, I owe obedience to my lord, the king. Besides, I am fully confident that he shall not overburden me. So thus I find my comfort in Lionel who is young, strong, and bold. Him I want to retain for myself, for he is to wait on no one else but me. Now, dear daughter, tell me what you think about this."

Angeline whose grief made her unable to answer or talk to her father, finally recovered. She began, saying, "Oh dearest lord and father of my heart, it is impossible for me to advise you little or much in that matter, for I know well that you would not heed my advice even if I should tell you what my heart wishes and desires, namely, that you stay at home—which would be my greatest joy on earth. Nevertheless, it would become me even less to advise you to go to war and obey the king's message.

"Therefore, dearest lord and father of my heart, I shall recommend my plight to God and pray to Him from the bottom of my heart to preserve you in all ways possible. I wish to God that I could avert this war so that you, my dearest lord and father, might stay in your lands, that many others might go on living a quiet and peaceful life, and that many a widow and orphan might be spared much grief. This would be my greatest joy on earth."

"Oh Angeline, my dearest daughter," said the count, "I have no doubt at all that your heart speaks through your lips. Nevertheless, I am without doubt that there is one more matter that still distresses you, although you have not yet mentioned it to me; you have heard that I shall take Lionel with me as my lieutenant, and I know that his departure does not distress you little. But this should not worry you at all, for I am of good hope that his whole future depends on this war. Should he strive for knighthood—which I do not doubt—this would be his most likely chance to achieve it. Then I would be all the less likely to be berated for betrothing you to him. Who would not say, afterwards, that Lionel achieved the order of knighthood with his own hand and not through protection? Hence, he may have you as a wife in all fairness."

Now when the maiden Angeline heard these her father's words, she surmised well that matters stood exactly as her lord and father had stated, and thus she said: "Well then, since my dearest lord and father will have it no other way, I shall have to make a virtue out of necessity. But I beg you for the sake of all your love for me to take care of yourself as best as you can, and not to rely too much on fortune; for many a time has she shown herself very friendly only to hide a thousand dangers behind her back." These and similar words the count exchanged with his daughter.

But now it seemed to Angeline that it was time to take leave of her lord and father. She withdrew to her apartment with her two maidens, partly grieved and partly happy because she was well aware that her beloved Lionel stood highest in her father's favor.

CHAPTER LIV
🍎 *How the Count Had His Whole Household Called Together to Announce to Them His Intended Expedition, and to Order Everyone to Prepare Himself with the Utmost Speed. How Angeline Gave Lionel a Livery.*

The next day, the count ordered that all his retainers, noblemen or not, be summoned. This was promptly done according to his will. Now when they were all assembled together, he had the royal letter read to them, and thereafter he exhorted them most energetically to make themselves ready to the best of their ability so that he would not be regarded as negligent by the king. At the same time, he announced that whoever was in want of a horse, armor, or other gear, should report to the master-of-arms to be supplied in the best way possible. All told, they received this message with great joy, for every one of them was convinced of bringing back honor and booty from this campaign. The count had all his retainers dressed in new clothes from head to toe, all in the same color and style.

Angeline very artfully embroidered with gold pearls splendid liveries both for her father and for Lionel. Now when they had been wrought, she sent for Lionel, gave him both liveries and said: "Accept these liveries from me, my beloved, one for you and one for my dear lord and father. Think of me every hour of every day and show yourself all the more manly and knightly for wearing yours. Also, be wary and overlook no small enemy, for many a time does it happen that a small one overcomes a big and mighty one, as many old stories have it. I beg you also, dearest Lionel, to watch faithfully over my lord and father so that no harm befall him. His age and his weakness are no secret to you; therefore, I commend him to your care. I have no dearer wish than to see him back, wearing this same livery and battle-dress, and that you, my dearest Lionel, achieve the order of knighthood in yours and return into my sight as a gallant knight. Ah! How then could there be any more happiness and good fortune for me in this earthly life."

"Dearest maiden of all," said Lionel, "I accept this gift of yours with great joy, and I promise you by the true and great love which I have borne you for so long—should my ride take the turn I hope—not to return to your sight unless I have good and genuine evidence of having accomplished one or more manly and knightly deeds. I also hope that your father will find me so deserving that he himself shall solicit from the king the order of knighthood for me."

"May that be God's wish," said Angeline, "for this was our very plan when we last said goodbye."

After they had spent several hours in modest discourse, Lionel deemed it time to take a cordial leave from his beloved maiden, so that he might prepare himself according to his needs. He went to his lord, the count, with his daughter's livery, at which the count took no little joy. Then the count sent for his master-of-arms, ordering him to provide Lionel with such horse, armor, and weapons as he himself would use on the ride. This was carried out according to his orders.

All his men prepared themselves so thoroughly in a few days that no prince appeared at the king's court with such a well-equipped and well-organized host, for which the other counts and lords praised him highly. Besides, none of them begrudged him the honor of commanding the horseguards.

CHAPTER LV

🌱 *How the Count Left with His Men; How Lionel Left behind His Beloved Angeline in Such Great Sorrow that She Fell Ill. How Walter Remained at the Court and Sent a Message to His Father.*

When time had taken its course and the day approached on which everyone was to appear in Lisbon, the count proclaimed in his lands that all those who had been ordered on the expedition were to appear at his court. No one stayed behind, but they all came, riding to the court at the appointed hour and day. The count then gave a princely banquet to which he invited all his subjects. With them he feasted, and then he asked them to be civil and friendly with one another during his absence, which every one of them willingly promised to do.

The whole court was filled with the sound of trumpets and war drums; there was a great neighing of horses in all the stables; armors were clanging everywhere; and everyone started to assemble. When Angeline saw the seriousness of the situation and that there was no more staying behind, she realized fully that her dearest lord and father was about to depart with Lionel, and she fell into a great sadness, worrying about nothing else but that Lionel should not come to pay her a visit before leaving. But she had not been waiting long when her father came her way, armed from head to toe and accompanied by Lionel.

"Angeline, my dear daughter," said the count, "all my men are here, and they are equipped most gallantly. It behooves me not, therefore, to tarry any longer. I beg you not to let our departure pain you, for I trust the Lord God that before long we shall have settled matters in such a way that we shall return home soon. I shall leave Walter here with you; I have ordered him to remain at court; he will be a loyal steward to you during my absence. Moreover, I leave you my page who will have to ride to and from the army so that you might be apprised at all times of how matters stand. Likewise, you are always to keep me posted as to how you fare. Forsooth, the heaviest cross that I have to bear is that I cannot see you every day. Herewith, my dear daughter, I commend you to the care of the Lord God. May he give you health everlasting! Farewell, my dear daughter."

With these words, the count withdrew from his daughter's presence, for he could not longer hold back his tears. Angeline was so grieved that she was a pitiful sight indeed. Lionel also was greatly distressed, so much so that he wished to be gone from her, too. He offered the maiden his hand and spoke to her thus: "Ah! My beloved, I beg you not to sorrow so much, or you will render your lord and father's journey so much more burdensome than it is already. Take comfort, you will certainly receive word from us at least once a month. God bless you, my beloved. I hope that in a short time we shall have the joy of seeing each other again."

"Oh Lionel," said Angeline, "you leave me in such great distress! I am afraid that my heart will break from sorrow, for now I see you ride off with my dear father toward your enemy, who will meet you weapon in hand and with great grimness. How could I be cheerful when my thoughts will dwell on this so often?"

"Take comfort, my beloved," said the young man, "we hope that fortune will be on our side so that we may slay our enemies like knights and return to our lands in great triumph."

Therewith, he embraced the maiden and turned away, greatly dejected.

Angeline was unable to utter another word, so painfully did she weep. She sat with her maidens in great sorrow until the departure was sounded and everyone mounted up. Meanwhile, the count sat on his steed, greeted his assembled men, and rode forth from the castle and through the city. Lionel was riding next to him, then the noblemen from all his lands, fully equipped with everything they needed. Then there arose among the commoners a wailing and weeping as wretched as if their lord were being carried to the grave.

Angeline posted herself at the highest window of her apartment so that she might gaze at the pageant all the longer. She sent after it her wishes for good luck and for a cheerful return. And when she could no longer distinguish anyone, she withdrew to her chamber and did nothing else all day long but sigh, lament, and weep, partaking of neither food nor drink until the next day.

Walter, however, rode with Lionel and conferred with him as to how he was to behave during his absence. He also gave Lionel a letter which he was to dispatch from Lisbon and have it delivered to his father in Salamanca, to apprise him of how he fared. "Otherwise," said Walter, "I know well that my father would greatly worry about me." Thus, Walter spent that night with Lionel.

In the morning they parted company, each riding his way: Walter back to court, and Lionel with the count to Lisbon, where they were received most magnificently by the king, for they came riding in beautiful array, a sight in which the king took no little joy. In a short time, arrangements were made and orders given to let everyone know what his assignment was. The people also kept the king posted day by day on the damage the king of Castile was wreaking, and on account of which they had solicited the help and support of the king of Portugal; and even if this help would be but slight, they would rout the enemy in a short time and drive him off in such a way that he would no longer enjoy being in Portugal, for they had ascertained that the enemy had no reserves. Moreover, the enemy was at a disadvantage, since they had no cavalry to support them. No sooner did the king receive this piece of intelligence than all his men were alerted and orders were issued to break camp in the morning. All this came to pass as the king had commanded.

CHAPTER LVI
🌂 *How the King Attacked the Castilians during the Night and How He Beat Them Most Severely.*

The king's men set forth with great joy. The enemy had posted sentinels in the mountain, but the Portuguese knew more passes and secret paths, and so they knew where all the sentinels stood. When the king of Portugal had heard all the intelligence reports, he very quietly led his infantry over the mountain range. But his cavalry he had stay at the foot of the mountain.

He marched the whole night in total silence and arrived behind the camp of his enemies. Beforehand, however, he had ordered the country people to form a separate body which was to attack the enemy's left flank. Then he split his own host in two groups, one of which he ordered to engage the enemy on the right flank. In addition, a great number of Portuguese peasants armed with slings and bows hid themselves in the woods unbeknownst to the foe.

When the king had been informed by signals and secret messengers that his plan was proceeding according to his wishes, he instructed the different hosts that they were to raise a frightful clamor, loudly beat the war drums and blow their trumpets when they attacked the enemy, which was to take place on three sides at once. But the cavalry was to remain in hiding most silently until the enemy crossed the mountain.

When this plan had been set up with the utmost luck, the Portuguese launched their attack amidst a great and frightful clamor, at which the enemy took no little fright. No matter to which side they turned, one of the two other hosts was driving into them from the rear, and, therefore, their only recourse was a frantic flight across the mountain. There they happened among the peasants lying in ambush. These pelted them heavily with stones and fearsome arrows. A counterattack was impossible under such conditions, and all that they could undertake was to flee with all their might.

Only after they had crossed the mountain did they venture to rally and offer resistance to their enemy; but this was to no avail, for now the cavalry broke against them with all its might. This onrush so dispirited the retreating foes that they had to ask for mercy, throwing away their arms and giving themselves up as prisoners without any resistance. Thus, there remained none of that host that had not been slain, wounded, or taken prisoner, from which the king gathered no little comfort. He hastily assembled his men so that he might also rout the enemy's main host.

When his men had eaten a fair meal, he gathered the whole host of them into a circle. Now when they were all assembled, the king first of all thanked them deeply for their manly and knightly victory, after which he strongly praised their wariness, and finally he exhorted them not to be idle but to press on and continue routing their enemies. Since these were still full of fear, great things might be achieved; but should the Portuguese waste any time, it was to be feared that the enemy might rally and then present a far greater danger than presently with their backs turned. This advice was to the liking of the Portuguese, who marched against the enemy forthwith.

The king of Castile commanded this host in person, and he led it in a most orderly fashion. Thus, the Portuguese had a harder task to accomplish than with the other host, and had the Castilians not been so few, the Portuguese would have been in great danger.

The two hosts joined battle. Since both sides knew that the other army was led by its king, they fought all the more gallantly. The horseguards fought very well on both sides, but since the Castilians had no reserves, they became quite weary from long and strenuous battle. Eventually, they attempted to retreat to their barricade of wagons.

Lionel noticed this before anyone else, and with some of the horseguards, he cut them off, thus forcing them back to the battle. When the king of Castile perceived what had happened and when he realized that his men were too few, he attempted to flee, but the count forestalled this wile and rushed at him with the whole host of his horseguards. Now when the king saw that his flight had failed, he quickly made for the barricade of wagons with the hope of finding shelter in it.

Lionel, however, charged the king all by himself and so forcefully that he toppled horse and rider with his couched spear. Now when the king realized that he had been overpowered, he asked for mercy and surrendered himself into Lionel's safe custody, immediately asking that peace be proclaimed, for he was concerned about his loyal warriors.

Thus, peace was proclaimed and the strife was ended to the great detriment of the Castilians. Lionel brought his captive before the king of Portugal, into whose hands he delivered him. The victorious king accepted the pledge of his defeated enemy as well as that of his men, whom he let depart after disarming them. However, he decided to take the king and those of his private council to Lisbon, and thus he set out for home with little loss, but with great booty.

CHAPTER LVII
🍂 How Lionel Is Dubbed a Knight in the Presence of the King of Castile, and How the Page Brings These Tidings to the Maiden Angeline.

The king of Portugal rode home in great triumph and joy, for he brought captive with him the enemy king and all of his councillors, whereby his whole kingdom had come to peace and quiet. As soon as he had entered his palace, the king had brought into his presence Lionel as well as the king of Castile and all the captive counselors. Now when they were all gathered, the king began to give an account of Lionel's whole life: how marvelous it was that he had been recognized by the lion Lotzman in his mother's womb, what manly and bold deeds he had accomplished so far, and also how his gallantry and foresight had set an end to this strife, wherefore it was only fair that he should be dubbed a knight.

He proceeded to do so immediately in the presence of them all, at which Lionel and his father-in-law-to-be, the count, rejoiced no little. The king also gave him weaponry and a splendid shield honorably emblazoned. Thus, Lionel was ennobled and dubbed a knight on the same day.

As soon as the page learned about these events, he hurried to his lord and begged him in a friendly manner to let him travel home so that he might inform Lady Angeline of all the events that had happened. The count was well pleased. At once he had a letter written to his daughter, which he sent to her by the boy, who did not waste any time on the roads. He constantly worried lest someone else get the better of him and earn the messenger's reward from the maiden, since he knew well with what sighing and longing she must be waiting for word from her father and Lionel. He made it to the count's court in but a few days.

As soon as he arrived, he dismounted and went in search of Lady Angeline. He was announced by her valet. "Ah!" said the maiden, "should the messenger bring anything but good tidings, don't admit him into my presence."

"Gracious lady," answered the valet, "all I can detect in him is that he is very happy and in high spirits."

"So bring him to me without delay, that I may learn how matters stand with my dear father and his men."

At once the youth was brought before the maiden. She received him with a most happy countenance and friendly words. The boy, however, as soon as he had performed his bow, blurted out: "Gracious lady, you owe me by right a good messenger's reward, for the tidings I have for you are happier than any you ever expected, namely that your father is alive and well, and that the war is completely over, for none other than your beloved Lionel took prisoner the king of Castile and delivered him to our lord the king, who promoted Lionel to great honor, for he ennobled him and dubbed him a knight on the same day in his palace in Lisbon. Of this, there is a thorough account in this letter."

There is no need to ask whether Angeline rejoiced at these tidings about Lionel. Everyone knows from experience what heartfelt joy the knowledge of a good friend's welfare can kindle. Therefore, I shall be silent about the joy that overcame the maiden: she had learned that her lord and father was still alive, that the whole country was at peace again, and, above all, that he whom she loved more than all the riches in the world had displayed such gallantry that he had achieved the order of knighthood and obtained great honor.

She took the letter, broke it open, and found that it bore out everything the boy had reported. Then she unlocked a beautiful box, took ten ducats out of it and offered them as messenger's reward to the boy who had brought her such good tidings.

CHAPTER LVIII
How Angeline Sent for Walter and Gave Him the Letter to Read; What Great Joy It Caused Him.

Angeline was extremely, unspeakably, happy. All her maidens rejoiced with her, especially Florence and Cordelia. She also sent for Walter, who came in great haste, for he thought some harm had befallen her. But as soon as he entered her apartment, she went toward him with great elation and received him cheerfully indeed. "Oh Walter," she said, "I have a great joy to share with you, for we received good tidings from my father." Therewith, she handed him the letter.

He read it from beginning to end, and it sent his heart soaring with joy. "Oh Angeline!" he said, "I tell you in all truth that this letter causes me more joy than the dream I had last night."

"What dream was that?" asked Angeline.

"I dreamt," said Walter, "that I had seen my dearest brother and companion Lionel in a great fray and skirmish, amidst his enemies. These were aiming forceful blows and shooting a great many deadly poisoned arrows at him, but he belabored them with great might and swift strokes. Finally, however, he vanished from my sight and the fight was over.

"Soon afterwards, I saw a young man wearing on his bare head nothing but a beautiful crown wrought of laurel branches; in his left hand he led some bound captive wearing a precious golden cuirass, his head covered with a gleaming helmet with lowered visor so that no one could recognize him. In his right hand the laurel-crowned figure held a naked sword gored with human blood.

"I gazed at him in all earnest and was convinced that I knew him, but his face was frightening to look upon, wherefore I forebore talking to him. Then, he passed by me with the prisoner and delivered him to the king. But in the end, this face caused me such great fear during my sleep that I fully awoke and lay the rest of the night in deep thoughts, pondering continuously how Lionel had vanished from my sight. But now I am quite satisfied by this letter, for if I lost Lionel from my sight, it is only because up to now I knew him as nothing else but a horseman, whereas now he has achieved the order of knighthood by dint of his sword and his manly hand. This is indicated by the laurel crown he wore on his head. Therefore, dearest lady, I justly rejoice at such tidings."

In the meantime, the page was walking throughout the whole court, looking for Walter from whom he also hoped to earn a messenger's reward. Finally, he was told that Walter was in Lady Angeline's apartment. "That means my plan has come to naught," he said, and now only did he announce his tidings to the other retainers.

His report ultimately reached the burghers in the city. These were overcome with great and exuberant joy when they learned that their dearest lord was alive and well, and bonfires were lit throughout the whole city. The burghers also dressed all in the same color so that on the day of their lord's return, they might ride out to meet him joyfully and in fine attire.

Now when the king had established a steady and perpetual alliance with the king of Castile, the latter was made to pay for all the costs of war before he was allowed to return to his country. Then the king of Portugal disbanded his troops, whereupon the count and his men returned home.

CHAPTER LIX
❦ How the Count Returned to His Lands with All His Nobles and Was Received with Great Jubilation by His Burghers as Well as by His Daughter.

You have heard about the great joy the count's people felt when they learned that their lord was alive and well. They attired themselves splendidly and marched out toward their lord, flying a small flag. But those among them who owned a horse rode toward him with a beautiful party of riders all dressed alike, at which the count took no little pleasure and joy, for he felt thereby how much his people loved him.

They reached the city amidst joy and jubilation. Now when Angeline heard that her father was arriving with her beloved knight, she and all the maidens arrayed themselves most magnificently and took up their stand to meet her father when he rode into the courtyard, receiving him most cheerfully and happily. Next came the knight Lionel, riding behind him with a steadfast and happy countenance. When he caught sight of his beloved maiden, he blushed deeply from great joy. No less did Angeline rejoice at his sight.

They dismounted from their horses at once and went into the great hall. There they took off their arms and their panoply of war. Before long, a number of tables was laid and everyone was seated according to his rank. What a princely meal had been prepared for that occasion! Angeline had everything prepared most sumptuously and ostentatiously, at which the count was greatly pleased.

There was no less joy in all the drinking places of the city, for the burghers and their wives had pooled their food and were spending their time together so cheerfully and happily that the count was greatly satisfied by it and offered all kinds of gifts and presents to the whole citizenry so that they might enjoy themselves all the more.

For several days, the castle was in great exultation, and court was held in grand style, for the count kept his whole baronage assembled for some time. But when everyone was well rested, they all rode back home with the permission of the count. The latter, however, entreated those sitting next to him to reappear at his court in about eight days, for he had a most pressing matter to settle. They all promised to return.

Thus, they all rode from the court. In the meantime, however, the count was busy with all the clothing, food, and drink required for a wedding, although nobody knew what was on his mind except Angeline and Lionel, the knight.

Now there happened to be in a town not far from the count's estate a baron who had also taken part in the expedition. He was a widower, so rich in possessions, lands, and people that he surpassed even the count in wealth. However, he was dishonest and prone to anger. When most had left the city, he tarried behind, staying at an inn, and on the following day, he forwarded to the count a marriage proposal for his daughter Angeline, which the count utterly rejected, informing him at the same time that he had already promised his daughter to a knight to whom he was to betroth her. At the same time, he thanked him kindly for his honorable proposal.

When the baron received this report, he waxed angry beyond measure but displayed no signs of anger so that he might avenge himself all the better. Now when he had learned by other means who the knight was to whom Angeline had been promised, he earnestly sought the death of that knight, but kept it secret so that he might jail him first. This intention, however, was reported to Lionel through a good and loyal friend, so that he might be on guard against the baron. Once the news had reached the ears of Lionel, the knight, he no longer rode into the city without wearing his good armor. However, he did not worry about this plot, unless the baron attacked him with stealth and cunning.

CHAPTER LX
How the Baron Attacked the Count, Walter, and Several of His Retainers; How Two of the Retainers Were Slain, Walter Taken Prisoner and the Count Bound to a Tree; but How They Were Delivered by Lionel.

Not to be accused of cowardice, Lionel, the knight, did not give any signs that he had been warned. One day the count and several of his retainers were riding to a castle he had not visited in some time. However, a Danish horse dealer had passed word of it to the baron who had wooed Angeline. The baron was also informed that the knight Lionel was to ride with his father-in-law-to-be, the count. The baron assembled a squad of horsemen without delay and ordered them to equip themselves with armor and weapons and to mount up at once for they were to perform a valiant deed of knighthood. All of this was carried out according to his orders, and in no time at all, he was at the head of ten horses.

The count had taken no precaution, for he had no knowledge of having an enemy, since he thought he was on good terms with all his neighbors. He took with him four of his retainers as well as Lionel and Walter, so that there were only seven who rode under his command.

The door to disaster was now opened when, after they had ridden half a mile or so, the count remembered that he had forgotten several letters that mattered a great deal to him. He did not want to order any of the retainers to fetch these letters, for he worried lest the matter be improperly handled; therefore, he ordered the knight Lionel to take care of it.

None of them wore any armor except the knight Lionel; and he dashed back quick and fast. But he had hardly left his companions when the baron attacked them at a crossroads in the forest and slew two of the count's men without any warning, calling out with a loud voice, "Surrender, all of you, or else you will suffer death at our hands this very day!"

The count was greatly dismayed by the lightning attack, especially since he had witnessed with his own eyes the swift death of his retainers, so that he was left with but two of them and Walter, and these feared exceedingly. There was not much to think about, for they were completely surrounded by armed horsemen. Therefore, they begged for mercy. The baron rushed at Walter, for the latter bore a likeness to Lionel. He ordered him and the two retainers of the count to be led away. The count, however, he had bound to a tree. He turned to him, saying: "Since you have preferred this peasant's son over me and given your daughter to him rather than to me, I shall leave you here for your shame."

At this point arrived knight Lionel. He noticed with one glance his lord bound to a tree and the baron still reviling him. He saw clearly that all was not well with his lord, who was in a dire plight. Since the baron threatened him, he forwent any ado but flung out his good sword anon and said: "Gracious lord, who inflicted this shame on you? Tell me and I shall avenge it with my knightly sword or lose my life for it."

The baron, who was a proud and vain man, recognized the knight at once and realized that he had captured the wrong man.

He told Lionel with great arrogance, "You peasant knight, nothing else and nothing better will befall you on this day, so let us not waste any time."

The knight swiftly raised his good sharp sword and aimed a forceful blow at the baron, who jerked his head out of the stroke's reach so that Lionel missed him, but cut deeply into his horse's head, wherefrom the animal waxed quite furious and galloped through the woods in great pain and anger. Lionel flew after it, bridle down, and remained on its heels until the steed began to weaken and floundered. Then the knight Lionel said with anger, "Lord, you had better surrender without delay, or else you shall leave me your life right here in this forest; and no one will spare you this."

The baron undertook to defend himself with violence, at the same time calling for his servants, but these were too far away from him. The knight Lionel waxed so furious against him that he no longer desired to take him prisoner; he delivered his blows with all his might until the lord grew so exhausted that he was unable to defend himself any longer and begged for mercy.

Thus, Lionel took him prisoner, but before he did so, he made him hand over his sword. Then he quickly led him back to his lord. There Lionel was informed of everything that had happened to the two retainers. His heart boiled over with anger and the baron had to take an oath and swear to follow the two of them. They led him to a nearby castle where Lionel expected to find his companion Walter and the two retainers, for he thought that his lord had sent them ahead and had been attacked only afterwards. But when he heard that Walter was a prisoner, he swore by his knighthood that he would neither rest nor pause until his companion was free and out of prison, and if such did not take place that same night, he was going to put the baron to death with his own hand. Since he told all this to the baron without witnesses, the latter was not a little dismayed. He immediately solicited paper, pen, and ink, so that he could write a letter at once and send it to his steward so that he would not throw the captives into the dungeon. His wish was granted at once.

CHAPTER LXI
🦌 *How Walter Was Freed and How Lionel Exacted Great Possessions from the Baron because of the Two Slain Retainers of the Count.*

When the baron had written the letter, Lionel did not let him close it. He read it first, for he worried that the villain was plotting more foul play and was secretly exhorting his men to treat him with violence. But since the letter was written to his satisfaction, he handed it back to the landlord, who sealed it immediately and sent it to his steward by means of Lionel. But before Lionel had ridden a mile into the forest, he came upon the retainers of the baron. These were glad of his arrival, for they believed that it was their lord who came trotting toward them through the thick forest. But as soon as they saw that it was not he, they were filled with fear, for some of them had dismounted and had taken off their breast plates. They had also bound Walter and the two servants to a tree to tease and badger them.

Lionel perceived this most clearly, for he had already caught sight of his dearest brother, Walter. He did not think about it twice but dashed among them with flying reins, and taking them to task, he cried full of anger: "You faithless and treacherous highway robbers you, tell me how you dare so shamefully take prisoner and tie up such a gentle lord on his own lands with violence and lawlessness, and also murder and kill so wretchedly his retainers who have done you no wrong. You had better surrender at once as your lord did or die by my knightly hand."

Therewith, he whipped out his sword and with all his might delivered a blow at one who wanted to reach for his breast plate, splitting his head halfway through the face so that he sank swiftly to the ground, dead. Immediately, he rushed at two more. With his first blow, he smote the head of the one off his shoulders and then struck his sword into the neck of the other one right through his gorget, so that he too fell to the ground, dead. Now when the others saw the stalwart and manly deeds of the knight, they were so frightened that they could no longer stand on their feet, but fell to their knees, asking for mercy.

Among these seven, there was also the steward to whom Lionel was to have brought the letter from the baron. When he heard that his lord had been taken prisoner, he feared exceedingly and immediately surrendered like the others. Then Lionel took their pledge and sent them on their way. But he kept the steward as his prisoner.

Walter and his two fellow prisoners were freed. They mounted their horses and began to rejoice greatly. "Oh, my dearest Lionel," said Walter, "had you not delivered us from that frightful situation, we would have been imprisoned in a deep dungeon, which this steward here promised us!"

"There is a way to treat those guests who reckon the bill without the innkeeper," said Lionel, "and this steward here will fare like him who digs a deep and fiendish pit and falls in it himself. Since he had made up his mind to perpetrate such an ignominy toward you who are innocent, he does not deserve any greater mercy from us, for I shall procure for him an even worse dungeon, which he well deserves for the way he treated you."

At these words, the steward was filled with fear and began apologizing profusely. As he was doing so, they arrived at the castle in which the baron was held prisoner. Lionel said to the baron: "Lord, you took prisoner my gracious lord on his own lands, and this against any right and public peace, and without any declaration of war; moreover, you slew two of his retainers before they could even defend themselves. Such behavior certainly does not become a nobleman, and you shall gain little fame for it wherever this shall be made known. But God would not stand for such a thing, for he never leaves any wrong unpunished: so He granted me to arrive in time to free my dearest lord and to take you prisoner instead. Moreover, you had taken prisoner my dearest companion. Him also have I freed, along with the remaining retainers of my lord. However I did so not with the help of your written letter, but with my knightly hand and good sword, as experienced by three of your retainers who lie in the forest, as dead as my lord's. All the others are my prisoners from today on and shall appear before me on an appointed day according to their pledge.

"But I have decided to keep in my power and custody your steward as the highest in rank so that I may ask a ransom from you. You have hated me because fortune favored me over you; I shall repay you for that by reporting you to his majesty the king, who shall avenge me."

At these words the baron was filled with fear, for he was not unaware of the knightly deeds Lionel had accomplished in the past war. He complied, therefore, quite willingly with the knight's ransom demand; he agreed readily to endure and suffer whatever Lionel imposed on him as long as the latter would not report him to the king and thus shame him.

CHAPTER LXII
How the Count Took Home the Captured Baron along with the Steward, and How Lionel Delivered Them Both to His Beloved, for Her to Deal with Them as She Saw Fit.

Upon these considerations, Lionel and the count bethought themselves that the castle in which they were at the time was not so strong after all, and they worried that the count's retainers, upon returning to their lands, would spread word about what had taken place and stir up some turmoil among the baron's peasantry, inciting them to free their lord with violence. Therefore, they did not waste any time but took the two prisoners under good escort and rode back home. As soon as they arrived at the court, everyone there wondered at the prisoners, for none had been aware of any enmity or strife.

As soon as word of these events reached Angeline, she betook herself to her father with all the maidens of her apartment. Immediately, the knight Lionel delivered his two prisoners to his beloved maiden, thereby informing her of all the circumstances of their capture. She marveled greatly at this and gave the order to lock up the two prisoners most securely until she had conferred sufficiently with her father and the knight. Armed men were detailed to watch over them.

Two days thereafter, the other retainers arrived and presented themselves to the knight as they had pledged in the forest. They were taken into custody in the same manner as their lord and in the same room. After Angeline had consulted with her father and Lionel, she released them, since they had carried out everything they did on the orders of their lord. The steward, however, had to stay with his master on account of his threats. His lord had to pay a ransom of one thousand ducats. At the same time, he had to give his solemn written promise of everlasting alliance and peace. He was also to treat the count or any of his household but with friendliness or in such a manner to which he was lawfully entitled. As for the steward, they ransomed him for fifty ducats.

The ransom was paid in a short time, and the baron had no objection whatsoever as long as he would not be reported to the king. And ever afterwards he behaved in such a friendly manner toward the count as well as toward the knight Lionel that one could not but greatly marvel at it. And after everything had been settled, he rode home with his steward. Now only did he bethink himself of how unfairly and how inimically he had assaulted the knight. Therefore, his ill feelings subsided.

CHAPTER LXIII

How the Wedding with Angeline Was Celebrated; What Joy It Occasioned amidst Tournaments and Dances.

Now when this strife was over, the count earnestly bethought himself that should he delay his daughter's marriage any longer, another lord might become unfriendly and make an attempt upon his life. So he prepared for her marriage as fast as possible. He ordered that there be hunts in all his forests and woods. And thus his subjects, low and high, eagerly employed themselves to that purpose, so that in a few days a great amount of game was gathered at the count's court; they also sent him large numbers of fowl, such as pheasants, partridges, quails, peacocks, heathcocks, and other birds.

On the wedding day the laden guests came in large numbers with their wives and daughters, clad in splendid attire. Everyone was received according to his rank and lineage, and the wedding was begun with great magnificence. But for the sake of brevity, I shall not describe it, for the only thing worth mentioning about it is that no expense was spared. The musicians and entertainers cost a goodly sum of money. Moreover, there were served up many grand banquets and court banquets of meat, fish, and fowl, dishes without number. And after every meal splendid and elaborate dances were held, in addition to which divers kinds of entertainments were provided; tournaments, races, fencing, wrestling, jumping, and divers other kinds of chivalrous games were performed for the pleasure of the beautiful ladies and maidens. The wedding festivities lasted several days, and never was there a shortage of entertainment or rejoicing. But enough said and written of this! Everyone may imagine for himself the glee and merrymaking that took place.

Now when the wedding festivities were over, everyone returned home. Lionel and Angeline lived together in good cheer, and Angeline found herself with child shortly afterwards, at which news everyone at the court rejoiced greatly, especially Lionel and the old count. When Angeline was close to the midpoint of her pregnancy, Lionel wanted to share his great joy and good fortune with his dear father and mother. He pondered night and day by what means he might make it known to them. Thus, he sought advice from his dearest companion, Walter, who consented to ride home and carry out his wishes in person.

So Walter set out and rode homewards by the shortest way possible, completing his trip in a few days. Let no one ask what great joy befell the tenant Erik and his wife when they learned that their son was blessed with such good fortune! Walter's parents rejoiced no less; Herman even decided to go and visit Lionel personally.

CHAPTER LXIV

🍎 *How Lionel Was Hunting with His Hunting Dog and the Lion, and How a Hart Wounded Him in the Thigh as He Pursued It with the Lion.*

Lionel was greatly enjoying life with his beloved Angeline; besides being profoundly godfearing, he often frolicked with his hunting dog and his lion in the merry green woods. Therein he stalked and slew many a head of big game with those two. One day when Lionel was engaged in his daily pursuit of big game in the woods with his hunting dog and his lion, they roused a mighty stag which the lion brought to bay. Lionel jumped from his horse, whipping out his boar hunting sword with which he meant to relieve the lion, for he worried that the stag might somehow harm him. But as soon as it saw the sword, the stag ignored the lion and attacked Lionel, goring him so severely in his right thigh with its sharp antlers that he began to bleed profusely. When the lion scented the blood, he quickly attacked the stag on one flank with great fury and tore it wide open so that it sank to the ground, dead.

Lionel, however, became faint from his loss of blood; he clambered back on his horse as well as he could and rode to a cool fountain to revive himself with its fresh water. Dismounting from his horse, he drew some water and took a cool drink so that he recovered his senses a little and was able to bind up and stop his wounds with wholesome medicinal herbs.

CHAPTER LXV

🌿 *How Lionel Was Found Lying by a Fountain by His Lord the Merchant and Walter.*

Just then it came to pass that his godfather, the merchant, came riding along with his son and took that very road through the forest where Lionel lay wounded near a fountain, unable to ride, stand, or walk because of the pain. Walter recognized his companion immediately but did not know how woefully he was off until Lionel informed him of everything that had happened with the stag. Lionel greeted his godfather cordially but from great pain could not ride with him. However, he entreated them to ride to the court and have a horse-litter sent out to him. They did not waste any time carrying out his wishes.

CHAPTER LXVI
❧ How Angeline Heard from the Merchant and His Son that Lionel Had Been Grievously Wounded by a Stag and How She Hurried Immediately to His Side.

The outcry that her beloved consort Lionel had been severely wounded by a stag and that he lay in the forest faint with great pain reached Angeline at once. Greatly frightened by this news, she grabbed a great many good and strong ointments and, refusing to wait for anyone, hastily took the road to the fountain on foot. There she found Lionel lying in a deep swoon, for he had lost much blood. Angeline was struck with great, heartfelt fear, for she worried deeply about her beloved husband. No matter how fervently she called him, he would give her no answer. Finally, her constant calls brought him back to his senses. He gazed at his beloved wife with a deep sigh and said: "Oh my beloved spouse, my heart feels so weak and so feeble!" Angeline comforted him as well as she could. She also quickened him with the good and strengthening confections she had brought along.

Just then, the merchant and Walter returned with a horse-litter; they also brought along with them a surgeon who began by staunching the flow of Lionel's blood; then he thoroughly dressed the wound. Thereupon, they lifted him onto the horse-litter. Angeline sat up in it with him, holding his head in her lap.

As soon as they reached the court, the old count was informed of the whole matter, and as he was hurrying down a flight of stairs in great fear, both his feet gave out, and since he was a man of big and heavy build, he tumbled down the stairs so hard that he was carried off as dead. Therefore a new grief arose at the court.

The count was carried into his room by his retainers and laid on his bed. Everything imaginable was tried on him, but quite in vain! Now when he realized that he was about to die, he strove to die like a Christian. He put his household in order as best he could in what time he had left. On the third day, however, he died quite blessedly and was buried by his family amidst great dole and mourning, being profusely bewept. But these events were kept from Lionel until he had recovered enough from his wound, as you will find out.

CHAPTER LXVII
❦ How Lionel Mourned Greatly for His Father-in-law, and How He Sent for His Father and Mother and Also for Some of His Brothers and Sisters; How the Merchant Rode Back Home with His Son.

The good care and nursing lavished on Lionel brought back his lost strength rapidly, and he recovered completely from his wound. But the death of his father-in-law was still kept from him until one day he took his wife to task about why the old lord never had come to visit him during his illness. Angeline was greatly afflicted indeed by these words and began to weep woefully and bitterly, telling Lionel everything that had happened. When he heard this, he was so sorely aggrieved that everyone worried lest he should fall even more severely and seriously ill than before. Therefore, the merchant and his son, as well as Angeline, comforted him as best as they could. All that Lionel complained about, however, was that he had not been able to see the old count once more before his end.

Finally, he decided to send for his father, as well as for his mother, both of whom were still living with several of his brothers and sisters on the holding about which he thought often, and where they still had to earn their living through hard work. Therefore, he quickly made arrangements, sending two of his most trusted retainers, who arrived there a few days later and delivered their message quite diligently. The two old people heartily rejoiced at the news.

They hastily sold for cash everything they had, cattle, fields and pastures, house and farm. Then only did the good Erik find out how rich he was, for he collected a fair livelihood in products and cash. He took leave of his good friends and neighbors and rode off in great joy with the retainers of his son. Now when they came to Lionel, he, his spouse, and their whole household received them very cheerfully.

Very shortly thereafter, the king's general council met and informed Lionel that since the good elderly lord had died from a chance mishap, it was now highly necessary that he, Lionel, swear allegiance and receive the investiture, since the county had fallen to his lot on account of his spouse.

Soon after he had done so, Lionel issued an ordinance to all towns, hamlets, and marketplaces, appointing for each a day on which he was to receive their oath of allegiance. All this came to pass within a few days.

Then Lionel organized the whole court in the best way possible. He also bade everyone of his household to honor and respect his father and mother and not to revere them any the less because they were poor and simple peasants, for after all he had received flesh and blood from them. But he himself was very grateful to God for elevating him to this high station, for otherwise, he would also have to search for his sustenance in the fields. "But God, in his merciful providence, let me reach this position so that now I may come to the assistance of my father and mother, which is my duty and everyone else's according to divine law, if we want to live long in the lands our Lord has given us. This he promised us in the Ten Commandments."

This and other speeches he delivered to his retainers, who complied with his order quite readily. The shepherd Erik and his wife were also held in high esteem by their son's wife, as well as by their son Lionel, who rejoiced greatly at their living with him.

Now when the merchant Herman had been with them a quarter of a year, he and his son took leave of Lionel. Walter, however, promised to be back shortly, for at Angeline's court there was a lovely maiden who was born of good noble descent but was very poor. Walter, however, had quite an inclination for her. He mentioned it to his companion Lionel, who rejoiced exceedingly at this news. Therefore, he promised Walter that should he come back to his lands, he would give her to him as wife and then appoint him as his steward, at which Walter was very happy and delighted. He rode home with his father but did not waste much time there; he settled his affairs so that he might return to Lionel, his dear brother, before long. When his father and mother grew aware of this, they surmised that never again would Walter leave Lionel. Therefore, they resolved to sell for cash everything they had and to move to Lionel's county. They never said one word about it to their son but wrote Lionel of their plan, at which he was overcome with no less joy than when his father and mother had come to live in his house.

CHAPTER LXVIII

🦚 *How the Merchant and His Wife Moved to Lionel's County; How Walter Took the Lovely Maiden as Wife.*

The merchant did not think it over very long; he settled all his affairs and turned over those of his debts which he could not collect himself to one of his good friends to whom he gave his proxy. When he had made himself quite ready for the road, he took his wife and drove off cheerfully. They lost no time on the roads and in a very few days arrived in Lionel's county, where their son lived. Their arrival rejoiced everyone, and they spent much time at the court in great joy and amidst all kinds of entertainment.

Soon afterwards, Lionel arranged for Walter to wed the lovely maiden. This came to pass with the consent of both sets of parents even though the maiden's father—although of good nobility—was quite poor. Besides, Walter was not money-mad as people often are. All he wanted was to be granted a gentle and modest maiden according to his heart. But such a lot never falls to a person unless granted by God, as Solomon clearly demonstrated. And it was granted to Walter.

The wedding was held at great expense, Lionel seeing to all of it. And as the celebration drew to an end—just as any earthly joy has an end, too—Lionel installed Walter in a splendid castle that yielded a sizeable income. He gave it to him as a fief. But he kept at his court, as his steward and secret advisor, his godfather, who was quite a wise man, besides being very kind and a father to the poor. Therefore, he advised Lionel at all times not to burden his subjects too heavily. Therefore he was held very dear and greatly respected by all the peasantry.

Would to God that such advisors were found more often at the courts of princes and lords who would be so inclined and partial to the poor! But, unfortunately, one finds more parasites and skinflints who try to fleece their lords' poor sheep, and who agitate, intrigue, and scheme to shear them all the more. But at times, such evil counselors get their just desserts, and then they fare like Ahitophel who was so deeply mortified that he hanged himself when his infamous advice was not heeded. Similarly fared King Rehoboam and his tyrannical counselors. These advised him to chastise his people with thorns and scorpions as his father Solomon had done with whips. But what happened to him? He lost several parts of his kingdom and was covered with ridicule and shame, along with his young counselors.

Now you heard in what manner and fashion Lionel started his reign, and also how he did nothing without wise and sound advice, wherefore everything he undertook succeeded well. He greatly honored his father and mother. To the poor, he showed much kindness, meted out great alms, and tried to achieve everything in goodness. He also forfeited all quarrels and strife.

For hunting, he had a great fancy and inclination, which were well served by his lion and his dog. He lived in good cheer and peace with Angeline, bringing up in the fear of God the children that were granted them. Therefore, from all sides, young and old, much happiness and felicity befell them until God called them out of this valley of tears and to eternal bliss—to which will come all those who abide by His will. To those—and to us, if God the Father, God the Son, and God the Holy Ghost assist us in attaining it—He will grant glory everlasting. Amen.

Printed in Strassburg by Jacob Frölich, MDLVII

SELECT BIBLIOGRAPHY

Baudinot, André. *Les écrivains alsaciens dans la littérature allemande.* Paris: F. Alcan, 1937. Pp. 22–23, 47, 48, 50–52.
Bobertag, Felix. "Analyse der Romane G. Wickrams und Proben aus den ältesten Drucken." *Schlesische Gesellschaft für vaterländische Cultur* (1873–74): 17–34.
Bobertag, Felix. *Geschichte des Romans und der ihm verwandten Dichtungsgattungen in Deutschland.* Vol. 1. Berlin: L. Simion, 1881. Pp. 44, 61, 77–78, 100–108, 135–36, 137, 233, 235–66, 270, 284–93.
Böcherdt, Hans-Heinrich. *Geschichte des Romans und der Novelle in Deutschland.* Leipzig: J. J. Weber, 1926. Pp. 96–99, 101.
Brentano, Clemens. *Der Goldfaden. Eine schöne alte Geschichte. Wieder herausgegeben von Clemens Brentano. Mit Vignetten.* Berlin: Rütten & Löning, 1957.
Dyrenfurth, Irène. *Geschichte des deutschen Jugendbuches.* 3d ed. Zürich: Atlantis-Verlag, 1967.
Ernst, Paul. "Jörg Wickram's Roman, *Der Goldfaden.*" *Jahrbuch der Paul Ernst Gesellschaft* (1942): 13–19.
Fauth, Gertrud. *Jörg Wickrams Romane.* Berlin: Walter de Gruyter & Co., 1916.
Frenzel, Herbert. "Jörg Wickram: Der Goldfaden." In *Daten deutscher Dichtung,* 3d ed. Köln: Kiepenhauer & Witsch, 1962. P. 73.
Friedrich, Wolfgang. "Bemerkungen zu den Romanen Georg Wickrams." *Wissenschaftliche Zeitschrift der Martin-Luther Universität Halle-Wittenberg* 10 (1961): 1037–42.
Gödecke, Karl. "Jörg Wickram aus Colmar." In *Grundriss zur Geschichte der deutschen Dichtung,* 2d ed. Dresden: Verlag von L. S. Ehlermann, 1886. Vol. II, pp. 458–65.
"Der Goldfaden." In *Kindler' Literaturlexikon.* Zürich: Kindler, 1964. Vol. III, cols. 976–77.
Grimm, Jakob and Ludwig. "Letter of January 1st, 1808, to Benecke." In *Briefe der Brüder Grimm an Friedrich Benecke aus den Jahren 1808–1829,* edited by Wilhelm Müller. Göttingen: Vandenhoek & Ruprecht, 1889. P. 4.
Grimm, Wilhelm. "Der Goldfaden. Eine schöne alte Geschichte, wieder herausgegeben von Clemens Brentano. Mit Vignetten." In *Kleinere Schriften von Wilhelm Grimm,* edited by Gustav Hinrichs. Berlin: Ferdinand Dummler, 1881. Pp. 261–65.

Gumbel, Hermann. *Deutsche Sonderrenaissance in deutscher Prosa: Strukturanalyse deutscher Prosa im 16. Jahrhundert.* Frankfurt: M. Diesterweg, 1930. Pp. 10, 46, 49, 50, 60, 61, 91, 95, 110–14, 123, 125, 126, 142, 143, 149, 151, 157, 163, 177, 190, 195, 225, 233, 238, 240, 243, 246, 247, 248, 252, 255, 261, 264, 268.

Hirtler, Franz. "Jörg Wickram, der Vater des deutschen Romans, um 1500 bis etwa 1562." *Mein Vaterland* 29 (1942): 332–35.

Holderith, Georges. "Jörg Wickram." In *Poètes et prosateurs d'Alsace, une anthologie.* Strasbourg: Istra, 1978. Pp. 36–39.

Jacobi, Reinhold. "Jörg Wickrams Romane. Interpretation unter besonderer Berücksichtigung der zeitgenössischen Erzählprosa." Dissertation, Bonn, 1970.

Kosch, Wilhelm, und Bruno Berger. "Wickram, Jörg, *Der Goldfaden.*" In *Deutsches Literatur Lexicon.* Bern and Munich: Francke Verlag, 1963. P. 485.

Lugowski, Clemens. *Die Form der Individualität im Roman. Studien zur inneren Struktur der früheren deutschen Prosaerzählung.* Berlin: Junker und Dunnhaupt, 1932. Pp. 42, 56–157, 178, 201.

Martini, Fritz. *Das Bauerntum im deutschen Schrifttum von den Anfängen bis zum 16. Jahrhundert.* Halle/Saale: Max Niemeyer, 1944. Pp. 357–58.

Matin-Ten Wolthuis, G. J. "*Der Goldfaden* des Jörg Wickram von Colmar." *Zeitschrift für deutsche Philologie* 87 (1968): 46–85.

Metz, Walter. "Jörg Wickram und die Anfänge des deutschen Romans im 16. Jahrhundert." Dissertation, Heidelberg, 1945.

Meucelin-Röser, Marianne-Auguste. *Studien zum Prosa-Stil Jörg Wickrams.* Freiburg/Breisgau: Rombach & Co., GmbH, 1952.

Müller, Günther. *Deutsche Dichtung von der Renaissance bis zum Ausgang des Barock.* Darmstatt: Hermann Gentner Verlag, 1957. Pp. 117, 149, 163–70, 172, 247.

Pascal, Roy. *German Literature in the 16th and 17th Centuries: Renaissance Reformation-Baroque.* London: Cresset, New York: Barnes & Noble, 1967.

Podleiszek, Franz, ed. *Anfänge des bürgerlichen Prosaromans in Deutschland.* Leipzig: Philip Reclam Junior, 1933. Pp. 7, 21, 23, 24, 156–301.

Rapp, Francis. *Les Lettres en Alsace à l'époque de l'Humanisme.* Publications de la Société Savante d'Alsace et des Régions de l'Est 8 (1962): 75–92.

Ritter, François. *L'Histoire de l'imprimerie alsacienne aux XVe et XVIe siècles.* Strasbourg: F. X. Leroux, 1955. P. 563.

Scherer, Wilhelm. *Die Anfänge des deutschen Prosaromans und Jörg*

Wickram von Colmar. Eine Kritik. Strassburg: K. J. Trübner, 1877.
Scherer, Wilhelm und Ottokar Lorenz. *Geschichte des Elsasses von den ältesten Zeiten bis auf die Gegenwart,* 3d ed. Berlin: Weidmann, 1866. Pp. 276–83, 550.
Schmidt, Erich. *Beiträge zur Geschichte der deutschen Literatur im Elsass. Zu Jörg Wickram.* Leipzig: n.p., 1879.
Spenle, Matthias. "Elsässische Bauern und Geistliche des 16. Jahrhunderts in der Darstellung des Colmarer Dichters Jörg Wickram." *Colmarer Jahrbuch* 4 (1938): 97–108.
Spriewald, Ingeborg. "Jörg Wickram und die Anfänge der realistischen Prosaerzählung in Deutschland." Dissertation, Potsdam, 1971.
Stöber, Auguste. "Georges Wickram, littérateur populaire de Colmar, au 16e siècle." *La Revue d'Alsace* (1894): 45–60.
Volkmann, Herbert. "Der deutsche Romantitel (1470–1770)." *Archiv für Geschichte des Buchwesens* 8 (1967): 1145–1324.
Weller, Martha. "Wickrams Romane in ihrer künstlerischen Entwicklung unter besonderer Berücksichtigung der Briefe." *Zeitschrift für deutsche Philologie* 64 (1939): 1–20.
Weydt, Günther. *Der deutsche Roman von der Renaissance und Reformation bis zu Goethes Tod.* Berlin: E. Schmidt, 1951. Cols. 2086–87.
Wieckenberg, Ernst Peter. *Zur Geschichte der Kapitelüberschrift im deutschen Roman vom 15. Jahrhundert bis zum Ausgang des Barock.* Göttingen: Vandenhöck & Ruprecht, 1969. P. 61.
Wolf, Herbert. "Humanistische Einflüsse in der Früh-protestantischen Literatur." *Welt und Wort* 20 (1970): 145–60.

JÖRG WICKRAM'S COLLECTED WORKS

Georg Wickrams Werke. 8 vols. Edited by Johannes Bolte and Willy Scheel. Tübingen: Bibliothek des litterarischen Vereins in Stuttgart, 1901–6.
Sämtliche Werke. Edited by Hans-Gert Roloff. Berlin: de Gruyter, 1967–.

EDITIONS OF *DER GOLDFADEN*

Der Goldfaden. Strassburg: Jacob Frölich, 1557.
Der Goldfaden. Frankfurt am Main: Weygan Han [ca. 1558–61].
Der Goldfaden. Frankfurt am Main: Weygand Hanen Erben, 1567–68.
Der Goldtfaden. Leipzig: Nicol Nerlich, 1602.
Der Goldtfaden. Basel: Johann Schröter, 1616.
Der Goldtfaden. Strassburg: Marx von der Heyden, 1626.
Der Goldtfaden. Nuremberg: Endter, 1663.
Der Goldtfaden. Nuremberg: n. p., 1665.
Der Goldfaden. Edited by Clemens Brentano. Heidelberg: Mohr und Zimmer, 1809.
"Der Goldfaden." In *Georg Wickrams Werke*, edited by Johannes Bolte. Tübingen: Bibliothek des literarischen Vereins in Stuttgart, 1901. Pp. 265–440.
Der Goldfaden. . . . Edited by Clemens Brentano. Munich: R. Piper & Co., 1905.
Der Goldfaden. Edited by Clemens Brentano. Munich: R. Piper & Co., 1920.
Der Goldfaden. Edited by Richard Elchinger. Munich: G. Hirth's Verlag, 1923.
Der Goldfaden. Wedel/Holstein: Alster Verlag, 1945.
Der Goldfaden. Edited by Eva Johanna Rubin. Munich: Obpacher, 1962.
Der Goldfaden. Edited by Clemens Brentano. Berlin: Rütten & Löning, 1963.
Der Goldtfaden. Vol. III of *Jörg Wickrams sämtliche Werke*, edited by Hans-Gert Roloff. Berlin: de Gruyter, 1968.
The Golden Thread. Translated by Pierre Kaufke. Pensacola: University of West Florida Press, 1991.